Sunshine State
1996-97

W9-BLY-645

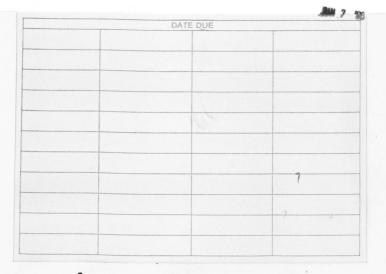

The

Grand

Escape

The

Grand Escape

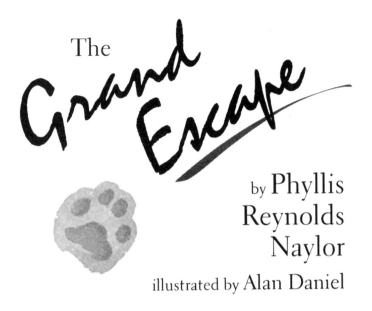

by Phyllis
Reynolds
Naylor

illustrated by Alan Daniel

ATHENEUM BOOKS FOR YOUNG READERS

Atheneum Books for Young Readers
An imprint of Simon & Schuster Children's
Publishing Division
1230 Avenue of the Americas
New York, New York 10020

Designed by Kimberly M. Adlerman
The text of this book is set in 12 point Goudy Old Style.
Printed in the United States of America
10   9   8   7   6   5

Library of Congress Cataloging-in-Publication Data
Naylor, Phyllis Reynolds.
   The grand escape/by Phyllis Reynolds Naylor. — 1st ed.
      p.   cm.
   Summary: After years of being strictly house cats, Marco and Polo
escape into the wonderful but dangerous outside world and are sent
on three challenging adventures by a group of cats known as the Club
of Mysteries.
   ISBN 0–689–31722–0
   [1. Cats—Fiction.   2. Adventure and adventurers—Fiction.]
I. Title.
PZ7.N24Gp   1993
[Fic]—dc20
                                                     91–40816

To Jonathan Lanman,
with gratitude,
and to Ulysses and Marco,
with patience

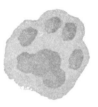

Contents

The

Grand Escape

1
How It All Began

During the icy blue days of winter and the spongy green mornings of spring and the steamy white heat of a summer afternoon, Marco had not especially wanted. But now that September was here, the air was dry and the sun still bright as it poured through the picture window, Marco wanted. It began as mild discomfort within his chest, settled into a faint flutter somewhere back in his throat, and emerged at last, an acute longing to be out.

"I'm going," he said from the velveteen basket.

"You say that every night," Polo complained, "and here we are, same as always."

"I used to mean someday; now I mean soon," Marco told him.

It never occurred to Mr. and Mrs. Neal that their cats could talk. Not only could they talk, but they spoke the English language. What other language would they know, Marco wondered, having been with the Neals since they were ten weeks old?

At first Marco thought his name was "Awww!" That's what people said when they picked him up as a kitten. It was later, when Mr. Neal began saying, "Marco, no!" or "Stop it, Polo!" that Marco figured out which name was whose. By the time they were fifteen weeks old, Marco and Polo had also learned the meaning of "Want a yummy?" "Let's have supper," and "Baaaad kitty!" Now that he was going on four years, Marco decided he had as good a vocabulary as any child in the neighborhood. Not only that, but he could read.

"I don't know how you learned reading," Polo would say with envy, when Marco jumped up on the counter to see if Mrs. Neal had added cat food to her shopping list.

"I simply paid attention," said Marco, meaning that all the time he was using the litter box with newspaper there at the bottom, he was studying the letters and words. He was bound to learn a little something. Polo simply did his business and climbed out.

The reason Mr. and Mrs. Neal did not know their pets could talk was that, when Marco and Polo conversed, it sounded like meowing. They could meow in hundreds of different ways that the Neals could not distinguish at all: soft and loud; short and long; wavy meows; sharp meows; meows that started out high and got low; meows that started out low and got high. Plus seventy-six different kinds of purrs.

"If we *did* escape, how would we do it?" Polo asked.

"Windows," Marco told him.

"Well, *I* was thinking of chimneys," Polo said.

"You could only climb up the chimney if the fireplace was open, and that only happens when there's a fire."

"But *you* could only get out a window if it was up, and then the screen is locked."

"So much for chimneys," Marco said. "So much for windows."

Marco was fatter and smarter than his brother. Polo was sleek and somewhat stupid, but he was quick. Very quick. Polo could jump from the mantel to the couch to the bookcase to the table, then run up and down stairs seven times without panting. Marco ran up and down stairs once and had to lie down. Both were gray-striped tabbies with yellow eyes.

They used to be content there in the Neal household, it's true, with no thought at all of leaving. Marco could still remember their first trip to the clinic for shots, and the vet telling the Neals that if they wanted happy, healthy cats, they should never, ever let them out.

"Hogwash," said an old orange cat in one corner, but of course, the vet hadn't heard.

"If they never go outside," the vet had continued, "you will never have cats meowing for you to open the door; you won't have to worry about their getting lost or run over; they will never get in a fight with other cats or bitten by dogs; they'll never get ear mites, fleas, or ticks. Keep them house cats, and they will be happy all their lives."

"Hogwash," came the voice again, but the Neals were already heading for the door, Marco and Polo with them.

So the Neals had made them house cats. But one day,

Marco and Polo were surprised to find the front door open wide.

Marco had thrust his nose out first, catching a whiff of trees and grass. Just as he and Polo set one paw on the doorstep, however—*splat!*—a gigantic waterfall descended from nowhere.

Terrified and dripping, the cats leaped backward and dashed behind the sofa where they sat shivering, licking their fur.

A few days later, however, the *back* door stood open.

"What do you think?" asked Polo. "*I'm* thinking I don't see any water out there today."

"But we didn't see any before," Marco reminded him. "It seemed as sunny and dry as it does right now."

They sat looking toward the door. For a moment or two, neither moved. It was Marco, however, who took the first step once again.

Slowly, slowly, with belly slung low to the floor, neck thrust out before him, and whiskers quivering, he crept stealthily forward, Polo only an inch behind. When the two cats got to the doorstep, they paused, sniffing the air. And finally, both together, each put out a paw.

Splat!

The waterfall came again. Marco and Polo rose up in fright and this time hid beneath the dining room table, wet and bedraggled.

"What do you think?" Polo asked.

"I'm thinking that every time we step outside, it rains," said Marco.

And so, when a few more days had passed, and the door stood open once again, neither of them budged.

4

Mrs. Neal walked about from room to room, straightening magazines and sofa pillows, humming and even turning her back, but Marco and Polo did not move. Finally, Mr. Neal came in from outside carrying a water pitcher, and Marco was actually relieved to see him close the door behind him.

So the first year had passed in the Neal household; during the second and third, Marco and Polo never crossed the doorstep. As the seasons went by—wind, snow, rain, sun; wind, snow, rain, sun—they sat looking out the picture window, their own TV. Marco's jaws trembled and he made little noises in his throat when a chickadee or nuthatch flew dipping and bobbing up to the bird feeder. Polo's tail lashed and he pounced at the window when a squirrel ran along the ledge outside, seemingly taunting him. But they did not meow to go out. They did not get into fights with other animals; they did not get lost or run over; they did not get fleas, ear mites, or ticks; and every time the door was left open for a few moments while the Neals carried the groceries inside, Marco and Polo stayed right where they were.

"Such *good* kitties!" Mrs. Neal would say to them.

"*Nice* cats!" Mr. Neal would say, scratching their heads.

So Marco and Polo settled down to become the house cats the Neals always wanted, and gave up all thought of ever going outside.

Things would have gone on like this forever, perhaps, except that two things happened. The first was that, on a fresh newspaper in the bottom of the litter box, there was a story about ranches. Marco read every word.

A ranch, it seemed, was a place where you could look for miles around you, and all you could see was earth and sky. A ranch was where animals grew sleek and fat, where the sun shone and breezes blew, and where you came home at night to a wonderful dinner—all you could eat, in fact. More than anything else, Marco wanted to visit a ranch.

The second thing that happened was that Mr. Neal went out one evening to bring in his stepladder and, having propped open the side door, forgot to close it once he got to the basement. Instead, he busied himself at his workbench, and the side door to the dark, sweet-smelling world beyond stayed open.

Marco was the first to find it. Polo was taking an early evening nap in the velveteen basket, but as Marco left the litter box in the laundry room, he came face-to-face with the great outdoors.

He sat down on the linoleum to think. He knew that walking out the *front* door made it rain, and walking out the *back* door made it rain, but he had never tried the side door. He wondered if he should go wake Polo, but if he did, he might lose his chance. Marco heard Mrs. Neal's footsteps in the kitchen as she prepared dinner. He heard Mr. Neal tinkering around in the basement.

Gingerly he crept toward the open door. A great swell of primitive longing rose up inside him, the cry of his ancestors, and his heart began to pound. He could see the sky beyond, turning purple in the evening dusk. He thrust his nose out. The smell of grass!

Slowly, slowly, Marco put out one paw and touched the doorstep, then jerked it back. Nothing happened.

7

He tried it again. This time he put his paw on the doorstep and kept it there. No waterfall. No rain. He put his other paw on the doorstep. Still no rain. And a moment later he was walking on grass for the very first time.

Marco would always remember it, a time like no other. Things felt different outdoors. They smelled different outdoors. Blades of grass moved before his eyes. Branches swayed. Toads hopped and lightning bugs flew. Marco went from one bush to another, his tail straight up in the air, quivering with anticipation. He sniffed and stared and pranced and even rested, for a moment, with his belly against the cool earth.

By the time the Neals discovered the door open and came looking for him, Marco had been outside for an hour, and he would never be the same again.

"Baaaaad kitty!" Mrs. Neal had said, shaking him when she should have been shaking her husband.

"You blew it, Marco!" Mr. Neal scolded. "No yummy for you tonight."

But it did not stop the wanting. From then on, when Marco sat by the window and watched the birds, he remembered the look of the sky when it was directly overhead, the sound of the wind as it went through the trees, the smell of a pinecone, the taste of a bug, the feel of moss beneath his paws. . . .

And that's how it all began—the Grand Escape.

"So when *are* we going?" Polo asked now from the velveteen basket.

"Soon," Marco answered. "Very, very soon."

2
POLO'S STORY

Polo too might have been happy forever inside the Neal home if something strange had not happened to him. Marco had told him all about his adventure, of course, and Polo listened, his large yellow eyes open wide.

But the nice thing about being stupid was that it didn't take a lot to entertain him. He found Marco's adventure absolutely fascinating. Polo could amuse himself by taking the pens on Mrs. Neal's desk in her study and carrying them, one at a time, to the living room. He could spend half an hour batting a pen cap around the hardwood floors, tossing it into the air with his paws, leaping and twisting, and chasing it under the bed.

Marco watched, looking bored.

Polo was always ready for play. If, when Mrs. Neal was changing the bed linen, she threw a sheet over Polo as he lay on the rug, then poked at him through the cloth, Polo would try to grab her finger.

If someone threw a sheet over Marco, he went to sleep.

Polo could have fun in an empty box or a laundry basket—with a Ping-Pong ball or a plastic straw. Catnip was the love of his life.

Marco liked catnip too, but after rolling around in it for a bit, his feet in the air, he realized just how ridiculous he looked, and he headed for the couch.

Polo still chased his tail. Every morning when Mr. Neal took his shower and the cats waited to be fed, Polo would go around in circles out in the hallway, trying to grab his tail.

"Why do you *do* that?" Marco asked once.

"Because it moves," Polo told him.

"So do your feet, and you don't chase them."

Polo thought and thought, but had no answer. After a while, he even forgot the question.

His favorite pastime, however, was not chasing his tail or batting a pen cap around or even playing with catnip. It was eating rubber bands. Not only rubber bands, but anything the least bit wiggly.

"It's disgusting," Marco said once as he watched a piece of string disappear into Polo's mouth. "Why do you eat that stuff?"

Again, Polo didn't know, except that it seemed to reach way back to when he was a kitten. Sometimes, especially when he had just awakened from a nap, Polo had a distant memory of looking for milk, smelling milk, feeling milk wet on his chin, tasting milk on his tongue. A memory of other little bodies crammed up against him, all wiggling—the sound of grunts and sighs and swallows. And from somewhere beyond the milk, like distant thunder, a great low purr. He tried to explain it once to Marco.

"That purr," said Marco, "was our mother."

If Marco said it, it must be so. Polo realized that he had no memory of their mother's face or whiskers or paws. Sometimes he almost, but not quite, could remember being licked with a long—very long—rough tongue; of having his ears cleaned as two strong paws held him firmly to the floor. And so he tried to put all these memories together—soft, warm, wiggle, purr, milk, tongue. If a soft-warm-wiggle-purr-milk-tongue ever wandered into the Neals' backyard and came up to the picture window, would he know who she was? If he said, "Mother!" would she remember? He didn't know. As much as Marco wanted to find a ranch, Polo wanted to find his mother, but thinking about it made him sad, so he sucked instead—the fringes on a rug, strings hanging from chairs, shoelaces, twine, and tinsel. Especially tinsel.

The Christmas of Polo's third year was almost his last. Mrs. Neal had set up a gift-wrapping station in the basement and arranged spools of crinkle ribbon on a curtain rod above the card table so that all she had to do was pull one end of the ribbon and the spool would unwind.

After she had gone upstairs, Polo jumped up on the card table. Four different colors of ribbon hung suspended there in front of him. The ends of each ribbon fluttered slightly, like something alive, just asking to be sucked and swallowed.

"Eenie, Meenie, Miny, Moe," said Polo, and chose the green ribbon. He snapped at the end until he had it

securely in his mouth, and began to swallow it down. It tasted as good as any wiggly thing he had ever eaten before, so he kept on eating, and the more he ate, the more there was.

After a while, of course, he began to feel full, and his jaws ached, but when he tried to walk away, the ribbon went with him. It was the strangest thing! He tried biting the ribbon in two, but that was difficult with his mouth full. And so he kept on eating and the spool went around and around, and it wasn't until he had reached the end of the ribbon that it snapped off and Polo was able to sit down and rest his jaws.

The next evening, the Christmas tree was up, and after the Neals had gone to bed, Polo stared at the hundreds and hundreds of glittering silver threads of tinsel. Marco had already gone to bed, after checking the names on the presents under the tree, but Polo's work had just begun.

He promised himself he would eat slowly, so he let each piece of tinsel tickle his nose once or twice before he caught the end in his mouth and swallowed it. One string of tinsel, metallic tasting, slid down his throat. Then another and another, like a big spaghetti supper.

When the Neals came down the next morning, they stopped and stared at the tree—at all the bare branches along the bottom. Then Polo yawned, and Mr. Neal said that his mouth looked like the inside of a tin cup. There were even bits of tinsel between his teeth, Polo could feel them. He was the only cat in the neighborhood with a metallic smile.

But in addition to the twelve yards of crinkle ribbon and the strands of tinsel, Polo discovered thin satin ribbons on the packages beneath the tree, a rubber band here and there, and a tassel on somebody's cap.

The day after Christmas, Polo did not eat his breakfast. He did not come when Mr. Neal offered a yummy. Mrs. Neal took his temperature, which, Polo decided, was the greatest indignity that could happen to a cat. But he was too sick to complain. The Neals took him to the vet, who felt a very large lump where his stomach should be.

"I'm sorry to tell you, but I think your cat has a tumor," he said.

Mrs. Neal cried and Mr. Neal looked sad, and it was agreed that yes, of course, Polo should have an operation to see if anything could be done to save him.

When he woke from his operation, Polo saw a glass bottle sitting beside his cage, with twelve yards of crinkly green ribbon in it, forty-seven strands of tinsel, a wad of string, eleven rubber bands, hair, a few satin ribbons, and the fringe off a rug. Everyone who walked by it said, "Look at that! Isn't it amazing what cats will put in their stomachs!"

When Polo came home, there were no rubber bands anywhere, no Christmas ribbon or tree with tinsel, no string. Mrs. Neal had even put away the pen caps. And when the bill arrived for the surgery, four hundred dollars plus X rays, the Neals seemed very upset.

"Imagine spending so much money on a cat, when it would have bought hundreds of meals for the starving people in Bangladesh," Mrs. Neal had said.

"If he does it again," said Mr. Neal, "the *cat* goes to Bangladesh."

"See what happens?" Marco told his brother. "Just because you miss Mom, you want to suck on everything that catches your eye. Once you suck on it, you want to chew it, and once you chew it, you have to swallow. Do you want to end up in Bangladesh with another seventeen stitches in your belly?"

Polo didn't know where Bangladesh was, but with no pen caps to play with, no string, no tinsel, no rubber bands, no ribbon or fringe, he went just a little bit crazy.

15

Every evening before dinner, he felt just a little bit wild. He would crouch down on his haunches, eyes huge, body quivering, tail lashing back and forth, and then he would *charrrrge!*

Up the back of the rocking chair and down again, across the back of the sofa, around the dining room table, up and down stairs—the silver bullet strikes again! Marco would sit straight up in their velveteen basket, ears perked, staring at his brother. *Galumph, galumph* went Polo's feet as he chased imaginary creatures from room to room. Then suddenly he would plop down on the cool stone of the hearth, panting, the crazies over for another day.

Because Marco was bored with being inside and Polo was half-crazy, they fought more than they had before. It used to be that when Polo wanted to share Marco's little patch of sunshine by the window or the warmth of the velveteen basket, he would ask permission by licking Marco's head and ears, and Marco would eventually allow him to lie down. But now they both seemed to want the whole square of sunshine or the velveteen basket. They would start to fight, and when the Neals came in the room later, there would be clumps of hair all over the rug.

"We've got to get out of here," Marco said at last. "That's all there is to it. We've got to find a ranch."

"We're both going nuts," agreed Polo.

And so it was one day, when the cats were sitting at the window watching the October sun turn the leaves of the maple yellow, that Marco said: "In the fall, Mr. Neal does a lot of work outside. He takes off the screens, washes the windows, fertilizes the lawn, rakes the leaves, and carries things in and out of the basement."

Polo listened.

"What we have to do," Marco continued, "is watch the side door. One of us has to be on duty all the time. Someday, Mr. Neal is going to prop open the door to carry something out, and when he does, we've got to be ready."

"What should I do if I find the door open?" Polo asked.

"Call me. All you have to say is, 'Marco, now!' and I'll come. When it happens, we've got to be quick. Out the door and no turning back."

"Where should we go once we're out?"

"There's a large bush just beyond the door. Hide in there until we can make a run for the fence," Marco said.

So every day the two cats took turns at guard duty. And one Sunday, around six in the evening, Mr. Neal propped open the side door a moment to bring in the lawn furniture.

"Now!" came Polo's voice from the laundry room.

In three seconds, the two striped tabbies were out the door and scooting under the bush just beyond.

3
Hiding Out

It was dark, damp, prickly, and smelly under the bush. A good kind of smelly. For Marco, it brought back wonderful memories of the hour he had spent in the yard on his own. But it was the first time that Polo's paws had touched bare ground.

"It smells like . . . like flower pots!" Polo said breathlessly.

"Earth," Marco told him.

"It feels like broom bristles!"

"Grass," said Marco.

"It's dark under here, like the inside of a box!"

"No," said Marco, "it's better. Being outdoors and on your own is about the best thing that can happen to a cat." He stopped talking suddenly. "Shhhh," he warned.

Mr. Neal was coming back across the yard.

"Don't make a sound, don't move a muscle, don't

wiggle a whisker, don't even breathe!" Marco warned his brother. "If he sees us, it means jail inside forever."

There was a rusty squeaking sound of a handle being turned, then footsteps again as Mr. Neal walked away, and finally a new sound that not even Marco could figure out—a soft, shushing, pit-pat sound.

Whoosh!

A spray of water landed on the bush, filtering down onto the two tabbies.

Polo's eyes grew huge; his body tensed, ready to spring, but Marco hissed again: "Don't move! Stay where you are."

And just as suddenly as the shower had descended on them, it was over.

"Whew!" said Polo. "I thought we were goners."

They could still hear the shushing sound, however. First the pit-pat sound grew fainter and fainter, then louder and louder, and *whoosh!* There it was again.

Polo closed his eyes and shivered. "Don't move!" came Marco's warning.

Once again the shower went away.

Footsteps. Mr. Neal was coming back to the side door.

"Uh-oh," Marco heard him say. "I left the door open! Lucky the cats didn't notice." He went inside and closed the screen.

Any minute he would discover them gone. Any minute he would come looking.

"See that shed next to the porch?" Marco whispered. "There's a space behind it where we could hide. When I say go, make a run for it."

The water was coming again. The pit-pat sounds were growing louder.

"Go!" Marco hissed, and the two tabbies streaked across the wet grass and disappeared behind the shed.

The space between the shed and the back porch was narrow and even darker than under the bush. It wasn't earth-dirty, it was dust-dirty, with cobwebs, old newspaper, dry leaves, sticks, spiders, and a broken clay pot.

Polo looked about himself in dismay. "*This* is what we were escaping to?" he asked.

"Only until the coast is clear," Marco said. "Do you see the trees out there in the yard?"

Polo nodded.

"Do you see the fence beyond the trees?"

"Yes."

"Beyond that fence is the whole world, and it's waiting just for us."

The side door opened, as Marco knew it would. "Are you *sure* they're not asleep on the dining room chairs?" came Mrs. Neal's voice.

"Positive. I looked everywhere. I can't believe I left that door open again."

"Oh, *Roger*! And it's getting dark out. They've already been fed too. Now they're certain to wander off."

"I'll get a flashlight," said Mr. Neal. A minute later a small circle of light began moving across the grass, followed by footsteps.

"Here, kitty-kitty-kitty!" came Mrs. Neal's high voice.

Marco had never realized it before, but Mrs. Neal sounded like a bird.

Then Mr. Neal was calling: "Marco! Polo! C'mon, cats! Dinner! Yummy time!"

"Who does he think he's kidding?" Marco whispered.

The circle of light came closer and closer to the tool shed. Mr. Neal even opened the door of the shed and looked inside. Then he went on.

"Here, kitty-kitty-kitty!" came Mrs. Neal's voice again as she walked along the back fence.

"Marco! Din-din! Polo! Yummy time!"

"How did we ever get adopted by such ridiculous people?" Marco murmured. "Why couldn't we have been adopted by a ranch?"

"What's a ranch?" asked Polo. "Tell me again."

"It's Christmas and birthdays and heaven all rolled up into one. It's sunrise and sunset and mountains and valleys and a horse to ride."

"What's a horse?" asked Polo.

"I don't know, but a ranch always has one."

They hushed as Mr. and Mrs. Neal came back toward the house.

"Well, I don't know anything else to do but wait them out," said Mr. Neal. "I'll never be able to see them in the dark. If I get the car out and go looking, I might run over one."

Mrs. Neal began to cry. "Roger, they don't even know enough to be *afraid* of cars. If Polo sees a squirrel, he'll take right after it, no matter where he is."

"Well, maybe someone will find them wandering around and call us."

"No one will know who they belong to! They don't

even have collars. Why would we put collars on cats that stay indoors?"

"This is wonderful!" Marco purred.

But Mrs. Neal was crying again, and neither cat liked to hear her cry. Polo swallowed. Then Marco swallowed.

"Let's put a dish of food outside the back door so if they get hungry, they won't starve," Mrs. Neal said.

"No!" said her husband. "If they get hungry and eat the food, they'll simply take off again! Don't worry so much, Jane. Maybe it's time they learned what the big wide world is all about."

The Neals went inside. The back door closed behind them. The light in the laundry room went off, and the square of yellow on the ground outside disappeared.

"Now?" asked Polo.

"It's probably a trick. They might be standing at the window in the dark looking out."

"When, then?"

"Wait until the kitchen light comes on. Then we'll go."

To entertain themselves while they passed the time, the cats told jokes:

"Knock, knock," said Marco.

"Who's there?" asked Polo.

"Cat-gut."

"Cat-gut who?"

"Cat-gut your tongue?" said Marco. "Ha-ha! Har-har!"

"I don't get it," said Polo.

"You never do," Marco told him.

"Knock, knock," said Polo.

"Who's there?" asked Marco.

"Polo."

"Polo who?"

There was a pause. "Just me," said Polo finally.

Marco closed his eyes. "Forget it," he said.

They recited all the poems they knew—"The Owl and the Pussy-cat," "Three Little Kittens"—and when they finally ran out of jokes and poems, the side door opened again.

"Here, kitty-kitty-kitty!" Mrs. Neal called one more time. But when Marco and Polo still didn't come, she closed the door and the cats heard it lock.

The light went on in the kitchen and a little square of yellow appeared far out on the grass.

"Now?" asked Polo.

"Now!" Marco told him. "Make a run for the trees."

They took out across the lawn and darted behind the trees at the very back.

"Follow me," said Marco, running along the fence. "There's a hole around here somewhere. I remember."

He found it and wriggled through, Polo after him. Free at last!

4

Life beyond the Fence

Is this a ranch?" Polo asked, staring at the darkness around him.

"I don't think so," said Marco. "Let's just see what there is to see."

There was everything to see. Everything was new and unexplored. Trash cans, weeds, rocks, boxes . . .

For several minutes Marco and Polo just sniffed. There were odors they had never smelled before, never even imagined. Damp smells, sour smells, sweet smells, strong smells. Smells that reminded them of things long forgotten—scents that reminded Polo of their mother.

He snapped at a long blade of grass waving just under his nose, and felt a sharp rap from Marco's paw.

"If you start that, we're lost," Marco told him. "If you fill your stomach with junk, you can kiss the world good-bye. There's no one out here to take you to the vet. No one to make you well."

Polo looked at the blade of grass longingly, then turned away.

Inch by inch, they started down the alley, their bodies stretched like rubber bands, necks thrust out before them, tails sticking straight out behind, bellies almost scraping the ground.

"Pssst!" said Polo suddenly, and Marco rose straight up in the air.

"Don't *do* that!" Marco scolded.

"But I *see* something!"

"What?"

"Eyes."

Something darted out from behind a trash can, and instantly Polo was after it. A second later, a mouse was trapped securely in his claws.

"What is it?" Polo asked curiously, staring at the mouse, who was holding very, very still.

"I think it's a mouse," Marco said, coming over.

"I *am* a mouse, you big lunkhead," said the small creature. "Take it easy, will you?"

"He speaks English!" said Polo, amazed.

"Of course I speak English. I lived in a house for two years and sat under the kitchen sink every morning while the family had breakfast. Look, if you're going to eat me, get it over with. If you're not, I've got business to attend to."

"*Eat* him?" Polo gasped. "Alive?"

"I taste terrible going down," the mouse added.

"Do *you* want him?" Polo asked his brother.

"Only if I were on a desert island and starving," said Marco. "Can you imagine how his whiskers would feel in your mouth?"

"Tails are worse," said the mouse. "It takes forever to swallow a tail. First it slides all the way back on your tongue, then it starts down your throat, an inch at a time. . . ."

Polo gagged and lifted one paw, and in a split second the mouse had scampered off.

Impatient to be going, Marco hopped up on a garbage can and motioned Polo up beside him. "We have to make a decision," he said. "Which way shall we go: north, south, east, or west?"

Behind them, they could hear cars racing back and forth. To one side was the Neals' house, to the other, more houses, and straight ahead there were lights and noise and music.

"What do we get if we go north?" Polo asked.

"Snow and ice and Santa Claus," Marco told him.

"What do we get if we go south?"

"Swamp grass and alligators," said Marco, never having seen an alligator in his life, only having read about them.

"What do we get if we go east?"

"The ocean."

"What do we get if we go west?"

Marco smiled wistfully. "A ranch."

"And which way is west?"

"That way, I think," said Marco, pointing straight ahead, so they set off for the lights and music.

It was a wee bit scary in the alley. There were noises Marco could not identify—rattles, scrapes, squeaks, and shuffles. But the light ahead became brighter still, the noise louder, and finally the weeds and trash cans gave way to concrete. The cats came out upon a huge parking lot, filled with cars and people. A red-and-yellow sign on a low building blinked on and off.

"Big Burger," Marco read.

"A ranch?" asked Polo.

"Use your head," said Marco. "You don't see any mountains, do you?"

The smell was absolutely delicious. Marco remembered that smell on days when the air was warm and the Neals left the windows open. It was like homemade bread and Cat Gourmet, all mixed up together, with a little fish, a little chicken, and maybe a spot or two of liver on the side. Just smelling it made Marco ravenous.

"I'm starving," he said.

"We just ate," Polo reminded him.

"That's the beauty of being on our own," Marco said. "We can eat again and again if we want to. We don't have to wait for someone to use a can opener. We can do whatever we want, *when* we want. We're *free!*"

They walked along the back of the parking lot until they came to the restaurant's trash cans. There, taking place before their very eyes, was a cat banquet.

At least a dozen cats of every description were feasting. They were on top of the garbage cans, beside the cans, *in* the cans. Marco could see a tail or two sticking up over the tops.

Every so often the back door of the Big Burger would

open, the cats would scatter, a man would dump another load of bottles, bits and pieces into one of the cans, and—after he left—the cats would come running back.

"Hog heaven!" said Marco, and headed for a piece of fish sandwich that was lying off to one side.

Just as he was about to take it, a huge paw reached out and swiped him across the nose.

"What do you think *you're* doing?" asked a large yellow cat with a white belly. "This is my territory and nobody eats here unless I invite him."

He was a huge cat, and Marco decided he had better be polite.

"May we join you?" he asked.

"No," said the yellow cat, then threw back his head, laughing, and the others joined in.

"What do we have to do to be invited?" Marco asked.

"Say the password." The yellow cat grinned.

"What *is* the password?" asked Polo.

"That's for us to know and you to find out," said the yellow cat. All the cats laughed again. Black and white heads poked up out of the garbage cans, grinning; striped cats opened their mouths and howled. Spotted kittens positively shrieked. Picking up the fish sandwich himself and holding it between his teeth, the yellow cat waved it under Marco's nose, then gobbled it down.

It was too much for Marco. He suddenly wanted that sandwich more than anything else in the world. He reached out a paw for the one small crumb left behind, and suddenly the fur was flying. A whirlwind of whiskers, tails, and paws went rolling across the parking lot as the big cat and Marco tumbled.

30

"*Get* him, T. J.!" the other cats chorused.

"Go, Marco, go!" whispered Polo, off to one side by himself.

The whirlwind fell apart, and Marco and the big cat stood up, their fur bristling, ears laid back, tails thumping against the ground.

A low growl came from Marco's throat—a terrible noise that Polo had never heard before. An even more awful noise came from the yellow cat with the white belly. People walking along the sidewalk stopped to watch. And then the whirlwind began again as the big cat lunged at Marco, and Marco lunged at the yellow cat. They went rolling and tumbling, biting and clawing, across the lot.

The back door of the Big Burger opened and out came the cook in his white apron and cap. He picked up the hose by the garbage cans and directed a stream of water into the heat of the battle.

Instantly cats flew in all directions. The yellow cat sprang up on a fence, the cats on the garbage cans went sailing into the bushes, Marco headed for the alley where Polo had disappeared, and a moment later there wasn't a cat in sight.

"Marco?" whispered Polo when he saw that his brother was limping. "Are you all right?"

Marco groaned. "Am I all in one piece? Are my ears still there? What about my tail?"

"Nothing looks broken, but I thought it was the end of you for sure," Polo told him.

They watched from the shadows as the other cats crept back to the trash cans and began feasting again. Polo, who had not been hungry before, now felt hungrier than he had ever imagined he could be. Every time he took a breath, his stomach rumbled.

"Who do you suppose he is?" asked Polo finally, as they watched the big yellow cat enjoying his dinner.

"The King, the Boss, the Cat Supreme, who do you think?" said Marco miserably.

For a long time Marco and Polo sat hunched over in the darkness of the alley, as the other cats ate their fish sandwiches. And then they were aware of a cat beside them, a smaller cat, a calico cat with three different colors of fur.

"Wait until they're full," the calico cat purred, "and after they leave, there will still be plenty left."

"What's his name, the big cat?" Marco asked.

"Texas Jake."

"What's *your* name?" asked Polo.

"Carlotta," she said.

5
CARLOTTA

The she-cat was right, because twenty minutes later the crowd of cats at the garbage cans had wandered off, leaving the feast to Marco, Polo, and their new friend.

The calico cat led the way. She was beautiful, with a coat of white, brown, and yellow that gleamed in the glow of the parking lot lights.

Marco had never gone to dinner with a she-cat before, and he wasn't sure of the proper manners. Polo just hopped up on the first trash can he came to, pushed his nose beneath the lid, and came up with a piece of hamburger. But Marco, having read a bit here and there, waited until Carlotta was seated on the middle can before he took his own place at the end of the row.

He cleared his throat. "Do you come here often?" he asked.

"I stop by every night, actually," Carlotta told him.

"What do you recommend?"

"The burgers are good, the cheeseburgers even better, but the fish sandwich is excellent. You really should try a little of everything, though. And save room for dessert. The fried apple pies, if you can find any, are delicious, and sometimes they're still warm."

Polo didn't have time for conversation. He was getting his first taste of french fries, and he had never eaten anything better. Think what he had been missing all those years behind the picture window in the Neals' dining room! He dived down into a trash can again, through the layers of cardboard and bottles, and came up at last with a bit of coleslaw draped over his nose. Marco was licking a dill pickle, and Polo decided he'd have to try that too. So much to eat, and so little time before his stomach was full!

Carlotta nibbled daintily at a piece of fried pie. "How long has it been since you boys ate?" she asked.

"A couple of hours," Marco told her.

"One would think you hadn't been fed for a year."

"Well, we've never had this," said Polo. "I've never even been outside until tonight." He told Carlotta all about the Grand Escape, and how brilliantly Marco had planned it.

"It's a whole new life out here," Carlotta agreed.

"How long ago did *you* escape?" Marco asked her.

"Oh, I don't have to escape. My master built a little door for me so I can go in and out whenever I please. I usually go out every night," she said.

Marco and Polo stared.

"Every night?" Marco exclaimed.

"Yes. I come home every morning—eat, sleep, let my master comb my hair—and then, at night, out I go."

"What do you *do* all night?" Polo asked her.

Carlotta smiled demurely. "Anything I please."

Marco simply could not believe it. How did a cat go about getting adopted by someone who would let you do anything you pleased? It sounded too good to be true.

"Do you live on a ranch?" he asked.

"What's a ranch?" said Carlotta.

"It's rather hard to explain," Marco told her, "but it's what we set out to find—a big place with mountains and valleys."

"I don't think I've seen one," said Carlotta. "I live in a house where I have my own basket with a brocade pillow and my own china dish. I have a ribboned collar to wear when company comes, a yellow litter box with a cover, and my own ivory flea comb. My master makes only one condition: I can't bring anything home. No birds, no mice, and especially no cats or kittens." She sniffed indignantly. "It's not a bit fair, you know. *He* brings friends home all the time. They bring in steak and wine, cook their dinner, and eat it in front of the fire. But if *I* bring home a friend and a bit of mouse or a couple of fish heads, maybe, you should hear him roar. That's why I can't take you home with me tomorrow morning and give you a place to sleep. But I can show you around the neighborhood if you like."

"Carlotta, you are a real friend," Marco said admiringly.

"I'm friends with a lot of cats," she purred, "but I like you because you're so new at this. When you've finished eating, we'll take a tour."

"We're finished," said Marco. "We can always come back later."

And so, with Carlotta in the lead, they walked out of the parking lot and down the sidewalk, three cats with their tails in the air.

"You have the perfect life," Polo purred.

"It has its drawbacks," Carlotta told them. "If you sleep all day and feast at night, you've really got to work

37

to keep your weight down. So I exercise a lot. Follow me." With that, the calico cat jumped up on top of a high fence and waited for the others to join her.

Polo hunched down, his hind legs quivering, and then, in a graceful leap, soared through the air and landed on the fence beside Carlotta.

Marco studied the fence. He had never leaped that high in his life. He had never jumped any higher than from the floor to a chair, and the chair to a bookcase. But there was Carlotta, waiting for him.

He crouched, wishing he had not eaten so many french fries, wishing that the calico cat would look the other way. "Come on, legs!" he whispered, eyes on the fence. He pushed off with all his might but didn't even come close. *Whump!* One fat cat smacking into one pine-board fence.

Marco lay on the ground, so embarrassed he could hardly stand it. His nose hurt. His head hurt. Even his whiskers hurt. But what hurt most of all was his pride.

Carlotta, however, simply waited. "Come on," she said. "Try again. If you can't fence-walk, you can't survive in this neighborhood."

"I think I ate a little too much," said Marco. But he knew that even if his stomach were empty, there was no way he could leap from the ground to the top of that fence without wings.

"There's a tree stump just down the sidewalk," Carlotta told him. "Get up on that and jump from there. I know you can do it."

So Marco launched himself from the tree stump, and even though he came to rest with his back legs hanging over one side of the fence and his front legs over the other, he made it.

"All it takes is a little practice," Carlotta told him. "Now we can sit here and clean up a bit. I always wash after eating."

"Oh, certainly," said Polo.

"By all means," Marco panted.

The three cats sat on the fence and licked and preened until there wasn't a taste or a whiff of a burger or a fish sandwich anywhere on them. Carlotta even leaned over and licked the top of Polo's head where his tongue wouldn't reach. Polo had never felt such pleasure.

"You know what I hate?" Carlotta said. "When people stroke me without asking. They think they're doing me such a favor, but it's always just after I've cleaned myself up. Then I have to wash all over again, every place they've touched."

Marco and Polo nodded.

"They don't realize how important it is to a cat to be purr-fectly free of any human smell whatsoever. Now, tell me about yourselves," she added, while Marco was putting the finishing touches on his tail.

"Well," said Polo, "we came from the animal shelter. At least, that's as far back as I can remember."

"Me too," said Carlotta.

"I *think* my mother was there, because I seem to remember a mother from *some*where. We were adopted by the Neals and would probably have been happy in their house forever if Marco hadn't got out one night when the side door was open and got a taste of life on the outside. Not to mention the fact that he reads."

"You can *read?*" Carlotta asked Marco in amazement. "*Everything?*"

"Well, almost everything."

"I can only read one thing," said Carlotta. " 'Beware of the Dog.' I learned to read that quick."

"That's how Marco learned about ranches," Polo went on. "By reading. Ranches with mountains and valleys and a horse."

"What's a horse?" asked Carlotta.

"That's one thing I never got straight. Something you ride, I think," Marco told her.

"Well, tonight we walk," Carlotta said. "I promised you a tour." And she stood up. "What you see before you is the street, and if you go out there you will probably get killed. You must never go into the street unless it is late at night or early in the morning and there are no cars coming at all. Now turn around."

The three cats turned their heads and looked in the other direction.

"What you see behind you is an alley. Alleys are streets for cats. Once in a while a car comes down them, so you do have to be careful, but mostly they are used for cats and dogs and garbagemen and occasionally a child on a skateboard."

Marco and Polo nodded.

"And all the rest," said Carlotta, waving one paw, "is the Neighborhood. If you learn its secrets, you can get around with your paws scarcely touching the ground."

Carlotta started off on their fence-walk, and Marco and Polo followed. One fence led to another. That fence led to a shed. Across the roof of the shed to the other side there was still another fence, and that one led to a garage. On and on they went, skittering up on a roof here, a fence there, a window ledge, a garbage can, until finally, dead ahead, was a large tree.

"Do we have to climb *that?*" asked Marco, wishing he were five pounds lighter.

"Only up to the first branch and down the other side," Carlotta told him, and after much huffing and puffing, Marco made it.

"I have something I must show you," the calico cat said, as Marco and Polo followed dutifully behind. There were so many turns that Polo was not sure he could find his way back to the Big Burger again. All at once Carlotta stopped, and her voice became a whisper: "Over there, behind that fence, is a place you must never, ever go."

Marco and Polo looked in wonder.

"Why?" breathed Marco.

"Because it's the home of Bertram the Bad."

Polo was shaking already. "W-w-who's that?"

"The biggest, fiercest dog on the block. A squirrel got in there once, and all that was left was his tail."

Marco swallowed.

"A rabbit tried a short cut and all that was left was a foot."

"G-g-gosh!" said Polo.

"If you ever hear that dog coming," said Carlotta, "if you even hear him *breathing*, run the other way."

Marco and Polo were both glad when she turned at that point and led them away from Bertram's yard, back

along the fences and across the sheds and up the big tree and down the other side until at last they were back to the Big Burger.

"Finally," Carlotta said, "and most important, cats do not have nine lives. You only have one life, and if you lose it, no more cat."

Polo thought he saw a tear in Carlotta's eye. He was sure of it when she turned her head away.

"Carlotta, what's wrong?" he asked.

"Sometimes," she said, sniffling, "I think about my kittens and get a little weepy."

"How many kittens have you had?" asked Marco gently.

"About eighteen, I think. Bertram the Bad got one, a car got another, a third wandered off, a fourth was drowned, and now, as fast as I have them, my owner gives them away. There's nothing as sad as losing a kitten before it even has a name." Carlotta lifted one paw and rubbed her face.

"Oh, Carlotta, please don't cry. I think you're wonderful," said Polo.

"Thank you," she said. "You're nice too, and I hope that someday you find the ranch and are happy forever."

"If we do," Marco promised, "we'll come back and get you."

With a flip of her tail, Carlotta set off along the fence to continue her solitary prowling, while Marco and Polo thought about where they would spend the night.

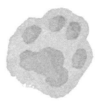

6
THE CLUB OF MYSTERIES

That was the one thing they had forgotten to ask Carlotta: where cats spent the night—cats that were not snug and warm in a home, that is.

"Maybe they don't sleep," Polo suggested. "Maybe they all stay home during the day and prowl at night."

Marco was thinking the same thing. But after four years in the Neal household, he and Polo were used to sleeping all night and half the day as well.

"We need some place warm," he said.

"And safe," said Polo.

"And dry," added Marco.

"And soft," Polo said. Preferably a place where there was milk and fur and a tongue. If ever his mother was going to show up, this would be a wonderful time.

The cats were not sure how long they walked, but it seemed to be blocks. They poked their noses in every doorway, every box, every hole, every trash can, looking for a place to sleep. Whatever they found was either too small, too hard, too cold, or taken. An October night was chillier than Marco had ever imagined, and the wind that seemed playful to cats that were inside a house—rattling the windows, whistling under the door—was crushingly cold when there was no velveteen basket handy.

Polo tried not to think about it, but the thought kept coming to mind: If they were home right now, Mr. Neal would be taking a small square box from the cupboard, shaking it a bit, and saying, "Well, boys, time for your bedtime yummy."

And Marco and Polo would rub up against his legs until he popped a Cat Gourmet treat into each of their mouths. They would drink a little fresh water from their bowl, stretch, do a slow, pushing-down kind of dance in their large velveteen basket, and finally go to sleep.

There would be no yummies tonight.

They had to settle for the hood of a car that was still warm. Huddled closely together, paws tucked under, they slept for only a short time, because the next thing they knew someone was yelling, "*Get* out of here!" and waving a newspaper at them.

Trembling, the cats returned to the alley once more.

"All we have to do," Marco said at last, "is stay awake till the sun comes up, and then we can find a warm place to stretch out. Maybe, with a little practice, we can learn to sleep by day and prowl at night, like Carlotta does."

They crouched between two trash cans to get out of the wind.

"Let's tell stories," Polo suggested.

"Good idea. You start."

"I don't know any," Polo said, which was just what Marco thought.

So Marco repeated all the stories he had heard Mrs. Neal tell her nephews, changing the characters around a bit to suit himself. There was "Puss in Boots," "Goldilocks and the Three Cats," "The Twelve Dancing Kittens," "Cat and the Beanstalk," and "The Fisherman and His Cat."

By dawn, Polo could scarcely hold his head up. Marco had just begun "Snow White and the Seven Cats," and had reached the point where the wicked queen disguised herself as a peddler, when he saw someone coming down the alley—someone stooped and bent, with a raggedy sack slung over one shoulder. Polo noticed too and crowded close to Marco as the figure came nearer and nearer. Then two big hands reached down where the cats were sitting, grabbed the garbage cans, and emptied them into the sack. It was only the trashman on his early-morning rounds.

Too hungry now to sleep, Marco and Polo went down the alley to the Big Burger restaurant and waited for bacon leftovers. They had to scrounge a bit but at last found a buttered biscuit, and had just begun to eat when they saw Texas Jake and his friends coming once again. They skittered back down the alley to wait for the sun to shine.

But the sun didn't shine. About eight o'clock, rain began to fall. It started as a shower at first, then came heavier and harder. It was colder than the waterfall that had drenched them when they tried going out the front and back doors. Colder than the water that had sprayed on them when they were hiding under the bush. What made this worse than either of the others was that the temperature had fallen, and a wind began to blow. Red and yellow leaves sailed through the air and made a slippery path underfoot.

The two cats took refuge at last beneath someone's back steps but had slept for only fifteen minutes when Polo jolted himself awake and nudged his brother.

Marco stirred. "Carlotta?" he murmured sleepily.

"No, it's me. Polo."

Marco opened one eye. "What's the matter?"

"Do you hear breathing?"

Marco lifted his head and listened. "Yes."

"What *is* it?"

"It's *you*!" said Marco.

"Oh," said Polo. He lay very quietly and breathed some more. That was it exactly! The sound of his own breath. He snuggled a bit closer to Marco and again they fell asleep, but not for long. An old gray tomcat hissed at them and ordered them out. He belonged there; they didn't.

By late morning, they were wet and cold and thoroughly miserable. They were hiding forlornly under the lid of a trash can when Carlotta, on her way home at last, found them.

"What have we here?" she said as she nudged off the lid. "Oh, no! This won't do. This won't do at all."

"We didn't know where else to go," Marco confessed. "Every place we found was taken."

"I'm going to check you into the club. Follow me,"

47

Carlotta said, leading the way to an old garage, and the two bedraggled cats were happy to obey. A *club*! Carlotta was a very high-class cat indeed!

Inside the garage, Carlotta took them up some leaf-strewn stairs. Marco congratulated himself on what a stroke of luck they had had in meeting Carlotta in the first place. When they stepped up into the dusty loft, two cats, who had been snoozing on an old army cot, opened their eyes.

"Boots and Elvis," said Carlotta, "may I present Marco and Polo."

Boots was a small white cat with brown at the end of his paws. He hissed, then wobbled to a sitting position. Elvis merely looked the newcomers over with his chin on his paws and gave a long, low growl. He was a medium-size cat, as black and shiny as a ripe olive. There was not a spot of white on him anywhere, his eyes were green, and just the way Carlotta had said his name made Marco a little jealous.

Carlotta, however, scolded Boots and Elvis for their bad manners. "Behave yourselves!" she said. "Marco and Polo have just run away, and I want you to treat them well."

At that moment, the floor creaked and suddenly a big yellow cat with a white belly rose up in one corner like the Goodyear blimp. And then Marco and Polo knew. They were in the lair of Texas Jake and his friends.

"Out! Out!" thundered the yellow cat.

Polo flattened himself on the floor and Marco felt the hair rising on his tail.

"Do you want me to finish you off right here or wait until later?" Texas growled.

"I'll give as good as I get," Marco hissed in return.

But as Texas Jake advanced, Carlotta swiped at him with her paw.

"Calm down, T. J.," she told him. "These are two friends of mine, in need of a good drying out. I see no reason why they can't share the loft with you; there's room for them and more besides."

Texas Jake looked as though he could *eat* Marco and Polo and more besides.

But Carlotta went on: "They need someone strong to look out for them, someone clever to show them around." She sidled up to Texas and touched his whiskers. "You'll do it for me, won't you, Texas?" she asked. The hair on his tail went down.

She strutted across the floor and nibbled Elvis's ear. The growling stopped. She nuzzled Boots's nose, and he nuzzled back.

"I want you to all get along together," she said. "If I find out you haven't, I shall be very cross indeed." Then, with a quick, "Ta-ta!" Carlotta disappeared out the door.

Polo would have preferred that she stay. With Carlotta out of sight, the other cats might butcher them there on the spot. He and Marco watched warily as Texas Jake exchanged glances with Boots and Elvis, and the low growling began again.

"I'm listening!" came Carlotta's voice from the stairs.

Finally the big cat climbed up on an old rocking chair without any rungs and began to lick his. fur, and that,

49

Marco knew, meant that he was going to settle down. A little, at least.

"It's only because of Carlotta I don't tear you limb from limb," T. J. said. "She has a rather delicate stomach."

Marco didn't reply. He was thinking that Texas Jake may be the Big Cheese, the Cat Surpreme, but Carlotta had a power over him he probably couldn't even explain himself.

At last T. J. peered over the edge of the rocker and looked the newcomers up and down.

"So why did you run away?" he asked.

"Because we'd never been outside," said Marco.

"What can you do?"

"Do?" asked Polo.

"Yes. Do. As in dig, dance, hunt, or howl. I, for example, fight."

"I watch," said Boots.

"*I* sing!" said Elvis, stretching himself out full length and admiring his own shiny coat.

Polo glanced at his brother. "Well, Marco reads!" he told the others.

The rest of the cats stared. The hair on Texas Jake's back began to rise again.

"Huh!" he said. "Well, what Carlotta didn't tell you is that this is the Club of Mysteries! *She* may think that all we do is lie about and sleep, but she's wrong."

Marco's eyes opened wide.

"Up here," Texas went on, "we discuss Life's Great Mysteries. No one can become a member until he has solved one of the Important Mysteries of Our Time."

Polo listened, very much impressed. After seeing Texas

51

Jake at the Big Burger, Polo had thought he was just a large cat with bad manners, but now he saw that Texas was, indeed, a cat of learning.

"What mysteries have you solved?" Marco asked the others.

"*I* solved the Mystery of Rain," said Boots, hopping down from the cot and stretching out full with his rump in the air. He gave a wide yawn, then sat down. " 'What makes it rain?' we used to ask each other. One morning it would be perfectly beautiful out—a wonderful day for cats to sun themselves—and the next there would be water pouring from the sky. That was the mystery *I* had to solve."

"I already know the answer to that," Marco told him. "Stepping out a front or back door makes it rain."

"Wrong!" said Boots. "Wrong! Wrong! Wrong! I step out of my own door several times a day and nothing happens."

Marco was amazed to hear this.

"So do I!" said Elvis.

"*Really*, Texas!" Boots said, turning to the big cat up on the rocker. "Can't we get members of a higher caliber than this? If we take in every stray that Carlotta drags in off the street, this club will go straight to the dogs, mark my words. Stepping outside has never, ever made it rain. A more ridiculous idea I never heard."

Marco was embarrassed. "Then . . . then what *does* make it rain?" he asked in a voice so soft that even Polo could hardly hear.

"Umbrellas," said Boots. "All you have to do is look out your window some morning. When men and women walk down the sidewalk without umbrellas, that means it will be fair. But if they are carrying umbrellas, folded or unfolded, you can bet your last whisker that before the day is out, it will rain."

Amazing, thought Marco. He felt a little in awe of such intelligence and wondered if he and Polo would be capable of solving a mystery of their own.

"What is the mystery *you* solved?" he asked Elvis.

"The Mystery of Hair," said the sleek black cat with the green eyes. "Did it ever occur to you that humans are the only creatures without a covering of some kind over their skin? Cats have fur, birds have feathers, fish have scales, but what do humans have? Nothing. Naked as a cat's nose."

"And did you find out why?" Polo asked respectfully.

"Indeed I did," said Elvis. "I discovered the answer in record time, if I do say so myself. It just came to me one morning when I was waiting for breakfast. The first thing my master does is take a shower. I always hang around when he dries to make sure he doesn't forget me, walk right in front of his feet when he goes downstairs so he'll know I'm there. And on that particular morning I realized that there are usually a few stray hairs at the bottom of the tub each time he showers. So I said to myself, 'That's *it*! The Mystery of Hair! All those showers simply wash the hair right off. It never has a chance to grow. If humans didn't take so many showers, they would be hairy as a rug.' "

Polo couldn't believe how smart these animals were. He thought of all the mornings he had been content just to chase his tail out in the hallway while Mr. Neal took his shower, when he could have been solving the Mystery of Hair.

There was a hush in the loft as all eyes turned to Texas Jake.

"What Great Mystery did *you* solve?" asked Marco softly.

Texas Jake stopped rocking and leaned forward, his big yellow eyes on the two cats before him. "The Mystery of Masters," he said. "The two-legged creatures control us coming and going. They tell us what we can eat, when we can eat, when to go out, when to go to the vet, but who tells *them* what to do? Who is the humans' master?"

Marco had never had a thought as deep as this. "Did . . . did you find out?" he asked.

The big yellow cat nodded. "Clocks," he said.

"Clocks?" exclaimed Marco and Polo together.

"What is the first thing your master looks at when he opens his eyes in the morning?" Texas Jake asked.

"The clock," said Marco.

"And what does he look at all through breakfast?"

"The clock," said Polo.

"What tells him when to eat, to sleep, and when to leave the house? The clock, always the clock," said Texas. "The clock is the Master Supreme."

"Gosh!" said Polo.

"I'd never have figured it out," Marco admitted.

This time the yellow cat leaned so far forward that he almost slid off the seat. "To join the Club of Mysteries," he said, "you each must solve a mystery that we will give you."

"Not fair! Not fair!" cried Boots. "They're brothers,

and they'll help each other out. Each of us had to solve a mystery by himself."

"True," said Texas, and he began to smile. "Then I shall have to give you one extra mystery to solve: three in all. Three Great Mysteries for admission to our club."

"That's fair," said Elvis.

"Absolutely," said Boots.

Marco swallowed. "What Great Mysteries do you want solved?"

"Now, that," said the big yellow cat, jumping down off the rocker, "I'll have to think about. I'll have to think about that a long time."

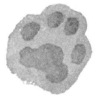

7
Boots's Complaints

When the club members set out later for the Big Burger, Marco and Polo tagged along. Surprisingly, Texas Jake did not try to stop them.

"Highly inappropriate!" complained Boots. "They don't even belong yet. Always before, it was just the three of us walking down the alley together."

But Texas Jake was all smiles now, and that bothered Marco almost as much as his growl. "Show a little generosity," T. J. said. "We're all brothers under the fur." He turned to Marco and Polo. "What'll it be, lads? Fillet of sole? Chicken nuggets? The sirloin supreme?" His voice was pleasant, a little *too* pleasant, Marco decided as he warily took a seat on the rim of a trash can.

"I'll go for the sirloin," said Marco.

"Nuggets for me," said Polo innocently.

Texas Jake rummaged through the cans until he found a bit of each and brought them over. Marco was more uneasy still at this attention. But as all the cats began to eat, with a great slurping and smacking, hunger got the best of him and he concentrated on the feast.

Polo was the first to finish, and he looked about with a satisfied smile on his face, licking his chops. Boots watched him.

"So you're house cats!" the small white cat with the brown paws said. "I used to be a house cat, and now—wham! Every day, every night, out the door I go. Rain, snow, sleet, hail—doesn't make a bit of difference to my mistress."

"Why does she put you out?" Marco asked.

By now all the cats had finished eating, and they climbed up on the wall behind the trash cans to groom themselves.

"A sad story of injustice, and it all began with hunger," Boots said. "Did you ever notice how humans eat anytime they want? Open the cupboard and get some crackers. Go to the refrigerator and get some cheese. A Danish in the middle of the morning. A little ice cream, maybe, around four."

He hunched down on top of the wall with only the brown tips of his paws visible. "And what did *I* get if my stomach rumbled between meals? 'Hush, Boots.' 'Not yet, Boots.' 'Two more hours till supper, Boots.' I tell you, I wasn't about to take that."

"So what did you do?" asked Polo.

"Helped myself. Got into the garbage after she went to bed, and she didn't like that at all, so she made sure she took it out each night."

"Then you behaved, right?"

"Wrong." Boots's eyes narrowed down to little green slits. "I was getting thinner and thinner and my mistress was getting fatter. One night she had a fancy dinner, but nobody bothered to feed me. Finally I couldn't stand it any longer. I leaped up on the table and made off with a breast of chicken."

"And nobody noticed?"

"Nobody would have if that woman hadn't screamed."

"What woman?" asked Polo.

"The one who got the wine in her lap."

"What wine?"

"The glass I spilled when I stepped in the scalloped potatoes. The next thing you know, the table was in an uproar, and I was out on my ear. That's the problem with humans. No loyalty at all."

"What I can't stand," said Elvis, "are the noises you can and can't make. I like to sing, but do you think anybody wants to hear? 'Shut up, Elvis.' 'Not now, Elvis.' 'Later, Elvis.' And then I'll be fast asleep in my bed, see, when they decide to have a party. People coming in one after another while I'm snoozing away. And suddenly my owner picks me up, sets me on the top of the piano, starts to play, and says, 'Sing, Elvis! You oughta hear him sing, everybody. Go on, Elvis. Let's have a little howl.' Can you imagine? Wake me up out of a sound sleep, don't even give me a chance to wash my whiskers, and here I am in front of twenty people, and I'm supposed to sing!"

"Shameful!" said Boots. "That's the way they are, all right."

A man came out of the Big Burger with a hose to wash down the trash cans, and headed toward the wall. So

Texas led the group back down the alley to the loft. Marco wondered whether he and Polo would be allowed back in again, but no one tried to stop them as they followed Texas up the stairs.

Each cat found a spot to settle down. Elvis and Boots hopped up on the army cot, Texas got the rocker, and Marco and Polo claimed the big bundle of old newspapers in the center of the floor. For a long time they were quiet. Marco was drifting off into sleep when Texas spoke.

"The worst . . . ," he began, and the other cats each opened one eye. "The worst is the way humans trick you into going to the vet."

That provoked such a spontaneous fit of howling that Texas had to lift one paw to regain order. "One at a time, lads, one at a time!"

"They wouldn't feed me all morning," Elvis told the others, his green eyes flashing. "And just when I was sure I would starve to death, they took a small bite of steak, dangled it in front of my nose, and tossed it into the very back of the cat-carry. The moment I went in after it—*zap!*"

"My mistress simply turned the cage on end, picked me up, and dropped me in headfirst," said Boots.

"The Neals always put us in a laundry basket, threw a coat over the top, and held it down," Polo confided.

"Well, my master put me in a gunnysack, closed the end, and I couldn't see a thing. Fought like a tiger, but he always won," Texas told them.

"It isn't fair," said Boots.

"Never was," said Texas Jake.

All that food and all that talk began to make them sleepy, and finally Boots dropped off to sleep, then Elvis, then Texas, and finally everyone was asleep but Marco.

Look at this, he said to himself. Only one day of freedom and already we've found a home. He began to think he might have been all wrong about the big yellow cat with the white belly. Perhaps Texas had not thought that he and Polo could measure up to the membership requirements of the club, but he was determined to do his very best at whatever task he was given. He stood up, circled a few times on top of the newspapers, then curled himself into a ball, and settled down for a long sleep.

They all must have slept a long time, because when Marco opened his eyes again, it was beginning to grow dark in the loft. He heard a dainty mew from the stairs, and then Carlotta's voice, saying, "Come on, you lazies! It's spaghetti night at the Big Burger. All you can eat."

The other cats woke and slowly roused themselves. Spaghetti didn't seem all that interesting to Marco, but, as the others explained, where there was spaghetti, there were meatballs, and all of a sudden, he wanted meatballs more than anything else in the world.

The alley was in shadow as the cats set off toward the restaurant. Carlotta and Elvis were walking side by side, rubbing their heads together and making soft little mews, stopping occasionally to lick.

But all of a sudden Marco, walking in front beside Texas Jake, came to a stop and stared. Because there on a telephone pole at the corner was a sheet of white paper, and in black marker were the words: LOST CATS.

The other cats stopped too.

"Lost," Marco read aloud. "Two gray-striped tabbies, four years old, Marco and Polo." Beneath that was the Neals' phone number, and below that, Mrs. Neal had drawn two cats' faces, looking very sad, with tears dropping from their eyes.

All six cats stared.

"Is that *us*?" Polo asked in astonishment.

Marco nodded, a smile creeping across his face. And before he could stop it, he was howling.

"They think we're lost!" he shrieked in merriment.

"They think we're sad!" Polo cried.

Then both cats together: "They actually think we *miss* them! Oh, ha-ha! Ha, ha, ha!"

"Isn't it wonderful . . . isn't it exquisitely delicious," Marco said, "to know that *they* are worried about *us* for a change?"

"Think of all the times our owners went on trips and we never knew whether they'd return at all," said Carlotta.

"Never knowing who would feed us," said Boots.

"Or change the litter," said Elvis.

"I think it is just amazing that Marco can read," said Carlotta. "And it's wonderful to see all you boys getting along so well together. I know that we are going to be the best of friends." She smiled sweetly at Marco and Polo. "If you ever want to thank me for introducing you to the others, you could bring me a mouse sometime—a young one. They're more tasty."

"You actually *eat* them?" asked Polo.

Carlotta licked her lips. "Every bite."

"Even the *tail?*"

"Especially the tail."

The only cat that hadn't spoken at all was Texas Jake, and as he started on down the alley beside Marco, he said, "You think you're smart just because you can read?"

"Not particularly," said Marco.

"Think you're wonderful just because Carlotta says so?"

"Not especially. We're just part of the club, like the rest of you."

"Not yet you're not," said Texas Jake, and his voice, once again, was a growl.

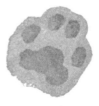

8

THE FIRST GREAT MYSTERY

Marco began to understand. And the more he understood, the more he worried.

If Texas Jake nudged Elvis to get out of his chair, Elvis would hiss at him, but he would move. If Boots had the chair and saw Texas coming, he was out of there in nothing flat. But as the big cat entered the parking lot of the Big Burger, Marco noticed, some of the neighborhood cats actually laid down on their backs with their paws in the air until the Top Dude, the Cat Supreme, had passed.

Marco had not turned over on his back when he met T. J. for the first time. He had not asked the big cat's permission to eat at the Big Burger at all. To make matters worse, Carlotta had taken him and Polo to the club after the fight with Texas, and now she had high praise for Marco's ability to read. The Top Dude, the Cat Supreme, the Big Cheese was not about to stand for this,

Marco was sure. Texas Jake was a fighter, and if he could not get rid of Marco and Polo one way, he would do it another.

Keep your eyes open, your ears pricked, and your claws ready, Marco told himself as he followed the yellow cat over to the trash cans and took his place.

The odd thing about dinner that evening was that all the other cats liked the meatballs, but Polo liked the spaghetti. There was something about those long, wiggly strands, draped over the edges of plates and cups in the trash cans, that reminded him of string and tinsel. While the others scrounged for a half-eaten meatball here and there, Polo attacked the spaghetti, snapping at each piece until he had it securely in his mouth and then, inch by inch, slurping, slopping, swallowing it down.

"Why does he do it, Marco?" Carlotta asked, when Marco told her about Polo's habit.

"He's looking for his mother," Marco told her.

"What?"

"It's really too complicated to explain."

Elvis was giving a performance that night on the wall behind the trash cans, so when dinner was over, the other cats settled down to watch. He cleaned himself first, while Carlotta groomed his ears, and when all was in order, he began with a few soft meows. He started out solo at first, with songs he had composed himself—songs like "Bertram Ain't Nothin' but an Old Hound Dog." Several people who were getting out of cars in the parking lot turned to listen.

After that Elvis was joined by some of the other cats

that came to the Big Burger for dinner—a Siamese with blue eyes that sang tenor, a Persian with a huge fluffy tail that sang baritone, and a large Abyssinian that sang a soft bass. They sang fast songs and slow songs, and love songs like "I Wanna Hold Your Paw."

To Marco, the song the cats sang next sounded very much like "America, the Beautiful," only Elvis called it "Ode to Cats, but Especially Carlotta":

How beau-tiful, Car-lot-ta's eyes,
How del-i-cate her ears.
Her voice—is ten-der when—she sighs,
She moves my heart to tears.

The back door of the Big Burger opened and a man came out. "Hey, cats! Knock it off!" he yelled, waving a towel at them. "Shoo!"

But the chorus was yet to come. More and more people were standing out in the parking lot now, pointing at the cats, and the cats—glad for an audience—tipped back their heads and yowled:

Oh, al-ley cats, oh, al-ley cats,
Our whiskers are so fine.
So raise—aloft,
Our heads—so soft,
And sing our song di-vine.

The man from the restaurant turned on the hose and started for the wall. This time the cats scattered in all

directions. He came after them, spraying their behinds with a stream of water, and a minute later Elvis, Carlotta, Texas, Boots, Marco, and Polo were scampering down the alley and into the safety of the garage.

Up in the loft they caught their breath.

"Oh, Elvis, you were magnificent!" Carlotta breathed. "I could listen to you all night."

"So could I," said Elvis. "My dream is to someday sing to an entire parking lot full of people. No man telling me to scram. No one coming at me with a hose. Just a parking lot full of people listening attentively from the hoods of their cars."

"It will happen, Elvis! Stay true to your dream," said Carlotta. "You were meant to be famous. You were meant to sing!"

Elvis gave a deep, satisfied purr.

But Texas Jake was sulking, and the first one who noticed was Carlotta. In an instant she rubbed against the leg of the rocking chair where Texas was sitting, and then she hopped up on the seat and began licking T. J.'s back. In a matter of minutes, Texas Jake's scowl was replaced by a smile of pleasure, and he stretched himself out, paws limp. But no sooner had Texas begun to purr than Boots looked grumpy, so Carlotta went over to him next and licked him under the chin.

Marco decided that he had been wrong about Carlotta and Elvis. She was a friend to many, but the true love of none. He wished Carlotta could be *his* one true love or, failing that, lick *him* under the chin. Just clean out his ears, maybe. But the cats were resting now after the chase down the alley, and he and Polo took their place on the bundle of newspapers. Soon they were all asleep.

Marco was not sure how long they had slept—whether minutes, hours, or days, but when he woke it was still dark, the loft was lit only by moonlight, and three pairs of eyes shown from out of the shadows.

He rose stiffly to a sitting position and looked around. He could just make out the shapes of Texas, Boots, and Elvis, all waiting, it seemed, all watching. Carlotta was still asleep. He nudged Polo uneasily.

Texas leaned down from the seat of the old rocker. "Well, well, well," he said. "Are we all dry and warm and comfy? Are our tummies full?"

"Yes, indeed!" said Polo, yawning. "Absolutely." But Marco's heart beat all the harder.

"Good!" Texas Jake told them. "Because you are about to receive your First Great Mystery."

Marco swallowed. Polo snapped to attention. Carlotta stirred and opened her eyes.

"Maybe you *can* read," Texas Jake said, looking straight at Marco, "but to solve the Three Great Mysteries we will give you, you also have to be fast and clever. Are you ready?"

Marco nodded. Polo nodded. The other cats crowded in closer.

"The First Great Mystery you have to solve is this: What is inside Bertram the Bad's doghouse?"

Polo thought his legs were going to give out from under him. Marco himself went a little pale around the whiskers.

"The boys and I," Texas went on, "have always noticed how Bertram barks whenever anyone comes near
his yard. He guards his house night and day, yet none of
us has ever seen what it is he protects so fiercely."

"Oh, Texas," Carlotta said worriedly, fully awake now.
"Don't you think this is a bit dangerous?"

"Nonsense. Polo is fast and Marco can *read*. A cat that
can reeeaaad," and here Texas drew out the word, "must
be a very extraordinary cat indeed. I'm sure that Marco
and Polo, being the adventurers they are, will have the
answer for us in no time."

We'll simply make a wild guess, Marco thought. No
way are we going to go inside that doghouse. They'll
never know.

But he was wrong.

"What we want you to do, in fact," Texas continued,
"is bring *back* whatever you find in that doghouse."

Polo almost lost his supper.

"I'll bet it's a diamond-encrusted collar," said Carlotta.

"Or a solid gold bone," guessed Boots.

"A silver-plated water dish, at the very least," said
Elvis.

Marco was frightened half out of his mind, but he had
to admit that it was a wonderful, terrible assignment. He
imagined returning to the loft to present Carlotta with a
diamond-encrusted collar. He imagined the other cats
gathered in the parking lot at the Big Burger while he
told the story of how he had risked life and limb to solve
the mystery. He imagined Texas Jake hating him even
more than he did now.

But Polo did not find the assignment exciting in the least. "Oh, Marco," he whispered. "We're done for. We're finished. We're dog meat."

"Only if we're scared," Marco whispered back. "Are we going to let Texas Jake make fools of us in front of Carlotta?"

"Yes," Polo whimpered.

"Are we going to have Texas, Boots, and Elvis calling us cowards behind our backs?"

"Yes," said Polo.

"Are we going to go back to the Neals and be locked in the laundry room for the rest of our natural lives?"

"N-n-no," said Polo. "But, Marco, what are we going to *do*?"

"Find out what's in Bertram's doghouse," said Marco.

"What's all the whispering about?" asked Texas Jake, from up on the rocker, and there was a sly smile on his face. "Not planning to run out on us, are you?"

"Of course not," said Marco. "We're thinking about the best time to go. Dawn, I figure."

Texas Jake nodded. "One of you has to attract Bertram's attention while the other goes inside his doghouse and takes whatever's there."

"You really have no right, you know," said Carlotta, still worried. "How would *you* feel if someone walked into *your* house and stole *your* pillow or basket or collar?"

"Did I say 'steal'?" asked Texas Jake. "Borrow, *of course*, borrow! All we want to do is see what it is Bertram's guarding." He smiled even wider. "After we've all had a good look, they can go put it back."

Marco tried not to listen. "Since you're the fastest,"

he said to Polo, "you'll have to get Bertram to chase you at the other end of the yard while I go inside the doghouse."

Polo could feel his heart thumping painfully and hoped that Carlotta could not see it pounding beneath his skin.

"What if there's a *Mrs.* Bertram in the doghouse?" Carlotta said.

In the darkness of the loft, the green and yellow eyes all focused on Marco again.

"Well, *is* there?" Marco asked. "Tell me everything you know about Bertram."

"He's loud," said Carlotta.

"And huge," said Elvis.

"And mean," answered Texas. "Other than that, we keep our distance."

"Till dawn then," said Marco. "We'd better get some sleep." He curled up on the pile of newspapers, Polo beside him, and though neither cat said anything, each could feel the other shaking like Jell-O.

It was still five hours before morning, and one by one the other cats fell asleep. But Polo lay with his eyes wide open. For four years, he and Marco had been protected from dogs and squirrels and wandering stray cats by the four walls of the Neals' home. Even when a German shepherd trotted into the backyard and came right up to the dining room window, breathing on the glass, the cats knew they were safe. Now, not only were they on the wrong side of the wall, they were going after the very thing the Neals had protected them from. Polo might not be the smartest cat in the world, but he wasn't the

71

stupidest either, and this was a dumb idea if he'd ever heard one.

"Marco," he whispered. "We could sneak out now, and no one would ever know."

But Marco was sound asleep. Carlotta was snuggled up against Elvis, Texas Jake was curled in a ball on the rocker, and Boots was on the floor now, lying on his side, his four brown paws out in front of him. He looked like a white cat that had been walking through mud. Polo tried to settle down on the bundle of newspapers and noticed it was tied with string.

String. He managed to get his teeth beneath it and nervously began to chew. It was comforting somehow. But the string was old and Polo's teeth were sharp, and after a while the string gave way and the newspapers began to slide. He slid one way, Marco slid the other, and so they spent the rest of the night, each on his own little island in the middle of the loft.

The morning dawned gray and misty, and the newspapers felt damp. Marco was the first one awake and hoped that he and Polo could slip off quietly to confront Bertram without a lot of advice from the others. But no sooner had he nudged Polo and managed to roll him over than he saw Texas looking down at him again from the rocker.

"Are we all rested and ready?" Texas Jake asked.

"We?" said Marco.

"What I thought," said Texas, "is that we could walk with you as far as the fence."

"We don't need any help," Marco told him.

But if Texas heard, he paid no attention. "Only as far

as the fence," he told the club members, and the other cats stretched and stirred themselves, rising sleepily up on their haunches.

And so, with the four cats following a respectable distance behind, Marco and Polo set out in the misty morning, along the tops of fences, from shed to shed, up and down a tree, from roof to roof, trash can to trash can. In the air above, birds watched and chirped warnings to each other, from tree to tree, pole to pole. At last, straight ahead, the cats saw the eight-foot fence that surrounded the yard of Bertram the Bad.

"Be brave," said Carlotta, kissing Marco on the nose.

"Be quick," she said, kissing Polo on the ear.

"Good-bye," said Texas, and the last thing Marco and Polo saw was his smile as he trotted off to find a safe place from which to watch a little farther down the alley. Marco and Polo stepped silently over onto the fence and sat looking down into the forbidden yard.

It was difficult at first to see through the fog, but in a while the cats' eyes were able to make out the shape of a doghouse in one corner. And then, they heard Bertram snore.

At first Marco and Polo thought it was thunder, or possibly a train, far off, going along the track, shaking the earth ever so slightly. But then they noticed that the noise came from the doghouse, that the fence beneath them was shaking, that their legs beneath their bodies were trembling, and that the big brown something sticking out the door of the doghouse was not a football, but one of Bertram's feet.

When Marco could speak at last, he whispered, "Here's what you do: Walk all around the top of the fence until you reach that corner way over there."

"Then I yowl, right?"

"Wrong," Marco said. "If you sit up on the fence and yowl, he will simply stand outside his doghouse and bark. You've got to climb down into the yard and let him chase you."

"Never to see sunlight again," said Polo. "Never to breathe the fresh air. Never to feel the taste of hamburger on my tongue, or milk in my bowl, or . . ."

"While I . . . ," Marco interrupted, "will *also* be down in the yard, doing something even *more* dangerous."

"I'm the one that's being chased, and *you're* the one in danger?"

"Yes, because you have a hundred ways to escape. If he comes after me while I'm in his doghouse, it's good-bye, Marco."

Polo began to cry.

"If *you* do a good job, however," Marco told him, "and keep him busy, I'll be able to grab whatever it is he's got in there. As soon as you see me climb back up the fence, follow. Don't stop until we've reached the loft. That doghouse is a little too close to the fence to suit me, and if he ever got up on top of it, he might be able to leap over."

The cats sat for a minute or two longer, getting up their courage. Finally Polo turned toward his brother, stared into his eyes for a long time, then quietly leaned forward. The cats touched noses, and Polo was gone.

Marco watched him grow smaller and smaller as Polo

went along the top of the fence, reaching the corner and starting along the other side. There was a lump in his throat. Did he really have any right to ask this of his brother? It had been his idea, after all, to leave home, and he was responsible for Polo. Would it be so awful if he just called the whole thing off? If they told Texas they weren't going to do it, didn't want to join the club? If they went back home to the Neals and had to spend the rest of their lives in the laundry room?

But he didn't call, and Polo didn't stop. Polo kept on going until he got as far away from Bertram's doghouse as he could. Then, ever so slowly, he made his way down the wooden fence until he was standing on the ground, a perfect target. He opened his mouth and gave a feeble "Mew."

The snoring inside the doghouse went on. Polo looked at Marco. Marco looked at Polo.

"Meow!" Polo said again, a fraction louder.

The snoring stopped, but the huge paw didn't budge.

Marco began to quiver and moved along the fence until he was right in back of the doghouse.

"Meow!" Polo cried, and suddenly the paw became a leg, the leg became a body, a head, a *noise*—and a huge brown mastiff, as big as a boxcar, burst out the door of the doghouse and thundered across the yard.

"Go, legs, go!" Polo told himself, and all his fear turned into one single, simple drive: to live. He dashed first one way, then another, the mastiff digging up the earth behind him as he came, the ground shaking, the huge dog's breath on Polo's hind legs.

Marco leaped down onto the roof, then to the ground, and into the darkness of the doghouse.

It smelled of dog. If Marco had more time, he would have stopped to count his blessings, one of them being that he was a cat, not a dog, but there was no time for thanks. In the shadows of the doghouse, he looked around for a diamond-encrusted collar, a solid gold bone, a silver-plated water dish. There was only something flat and gray lying in one corner, so Marco seized it with his teeth.

The ground was shaking again. No time to think; no time to lose. He tore outside as Polo streaked toward him. Together the cats leaped to the roof of the doghouse, then to the top of the fence, and with Bertram the Bad barking, bleating, and braying beneath them, they ran to the end, leaped to a shed, and were off toward the garage, the other four cats behind them.

Marco did not stop until he reached the loft. His sides heaved, his breath came fast. He dropped his trophy on the floor as Polo collapsed beside him and the other cats gathered around.

The valuable object that Bertram had been guarding so well was not encrusted with diamonds nor made of gold or silver. It was an old gray sock, tied in a knot, with teeth marks in the toe and heel.

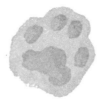

9

Dogs and Other Nasties

They couldn't quite believe it. The cats moved in closer, but not too close.

"This couldn't have been what was in his doghouse," said Texas. "You must not have gone inside, Marco."

"He did too, Texas. You jumped up on the fence and saw him yourself," Carlotta told him.

"It's dirty," said Boots, walking around and around the old sock.

"It smells," said Elvis, taking a wary sniff.

"That just goes to show," said Carlotta, "what you can expect from a dog."

Marco and Polo were still panting. Polo believed he was even more frightened now than he had been back in Bertram's yard. Now that he wasn't concentrating on his feet and keeping them moving, he gave his full attention to what might have been, and that was scarier by far.

"That close," he said to the other cats, holding his paws apart. "Bertram came just that close to catching me."

"Oh, Polo!" Carlotta said.

"I could feel his breath on my hind legs, his saliva on my tail."

"And I," said Marco, "could feel the ground shaking after I got inside his house. I didn't know where he was, whether I'd get out, or whether he would eat me alive."

Carlotta glared at Texas. "Well, T. J., you told them what to do and they did it, so you ought to be satisfied."

The cats studied the sock some more. Elvis flipped it over once or twice with his paw. It flopped disgustingly this way and that.

"They aren't very bright, you know," said Boots. "I used to sit at a window and watch the dog next door. Do you know what his owner gave him to play with? A bucket. That stupid dog would stick his nose in the bucket and run the thing around and around the yard. Sometimes the handle would flop down around his neck, and then he'd go about in circles trying to get the bucket off."

"If there's anything nasty in a yard, they have to roll in it," asked Elvis.

"If there's mud, they have to wade in it," said Texas.

"If it smells, they have to rub it over their whole body," said Carlotta. "When you're a dog, you must have to spend half your life in the bathtub."

There was quiet for a while in the loft.

"If they're dirty, stupid, noisy, and nasty, why do some two-leggeds prefer them over us?" Boots whined. "We

80

devote our lives to being well-groomed and particular, and what do we get? No gratitude at all."

"Well, dogs scare away burglars," said Texas.

"They run around in circles when their master comes home and jump up to lick his face," said Elvis.

"They lie with their heads in their owners' laps," said Carlotta. "If their master's happy, the dogs are happy. If the master's sad, the dogs are sad. But they might as well be puppets; they never have any minds of their own, while *cats* are—"

"—trustworthy, loyal, helpful, friendly, courteous, kind, obedient, cheerful, thrifty, brave, clean, and reverent," said Boots.

"Well, maybe not obedient," said Elvis, after a moment.

"Maybe not helpful," said Texas.

"Or loyal or trustworthy or especially reverent, but we *are* clean," said Carlotta. "And we all have to agree that cats—Marco and Polo anyway—are brave."

Nobody disagreed, but Polo noticed that Texas's tail began to swish. *Whup, whup, whup*, it went on the floor of the loft, thumping down hard each time it landed.

"That was only Mystery Number One," Texas said. "There are still two more to go."

"What's the next one?" asked Polo warily.

"I haven't decided yet," Texas told him.

Outside a light rain began to fall. The cats could hear it pinging against the window, tapping softly on the roof. It was a good day to stay indoors. Maybe they wouldn't even go home to their masters at all, Boots suggested. They all stretched out and lazily licked their paws.

"If you could be anything you wanted—even a two-legged—what would you choose?" Marco asked the others.

"Cat," said Boots.

"Cat," said Elvis.

"Cat," said Carlotta and Texas. "Naturally, a cat."

There was a noise down below, and Marco and Polo tensed, Marco half expecting Bertram the Bad to come after them, but the other cats hardly even stirred.

"It's only Mr. Murphy," Texas Jake explained. "Every morning he gets in his car and drives away. Every evening he comes home. But he never comes up here."

A car door opened. There was a long pause. The car door closed. Finally there was the sound of a motor starting up and a car backing out of the garage.

Marco continued the conversation: "Let's say that you could be anything else *except* a cat," he told the others. "*Then* what would you be?"

"Not a dog," said Polo.

"Not a mouse," said Carlotta.

"Not a bird," said Texas.

Marco was surprised at that. He had always fancied the way birds flew about so easily. "Not even a pigeon?" he asked.

"*Especially* a pigeon," said Texas.

"I don't think I would like to be a rabbit," mused Elvis. "Their ears are too long, not at all like mine—short, sleek, and exquisitely pointed."

"Maybe I'd be a squirrel," said Boots. "They don't smell or bark, and they can climb trees."

82

"We'll vote," said Texas. "All in favor of dogs?"

Nobody raised a paw.

"Mice?"

No takers.

"Birds?"

Marco voted for birds.

"Rabbits?" No votes.

"Squirrels?" The other five cats voted squirrels.

That decided, all six cats stretched out to sleep away the rainy morning. The rain was coming down heavier now, and when the wind blew, a torrent of water slashed against the window glass. Marco kept thinking there must be animals *some*where they hadn't thought of yet, but he couldn't remember any except rats, and those were so close to mice they weren't worth mentioning. No, he was quite sure of it. They had mentioned all the animals in the world besides cats.

It was drafty in the loft, and Marco and Polo snuggled up against each other for warmth. Carlotta and Texas were lying back to back, Elvis was on the other side of Carlotta with his head on her stomach, and Boots had found an old pillow in one corner.

For a long time the cats slept. Every time Polo woke, he thought of food. They had gone off to Bertram's that morning without a thing to eat, and every time he moved or turned over, he thought of french fries and catsup and cheeseburgers and hot apple pies. But every time he thought of going to the Big Burger in the rain, he rolled over and went to sleep again.

Everyone was up by noon, and everyone was hungry.

The rain had slacked off a bit, so they decided to chance it.

"Ready, set, *go!*" Texas said at the door of the garage, and the six cats streaked down the alley. As they passed the LOST CATS sign, Marco noticed that the rain had blurred the ink, and now it looked like a drawing of two cats with dirty faces.

The problem at the Big Burger was that business was slow, and there weren't a lot of people inside, meaning there were scarcely any leftovers in the trash cans.

"I think that Marco and Polo should have first choice for being so brave this morning!" Carlotta told the others, as they sat hunched on the wall in the drizzle.

Marco detected a low growl from somewhere down in Texas Jake's throat. If he hadn't been sitting quite so close, he might not have heard it at all. But it was definitely *not* a purr.

Elvis managed to get a lid off one of the trash cans and disappeared inside.

"One piece of quarter-pounder coming up," came his voice from the bottom of the can.

"I'll take that," said Polo.

There was more rummaging about in the trash can. "One bite of fish sandwich with tartar sauce," Elvis called.

"I'll take that!" said Texas.

"No, you won't!" Carlotta told him. "Marco gets that."

This time Marco was *sure* he heard a growl, but he didn't care. He was too hungry. Bit by bit, Elvis came up

84

with some other leftovers to eat, until finally every cat had a little something in his or her stomach.

"Fish," said Marco suddenly, swallowing his last nibble of sandwich. The cats stopped chewing and looked at him. "That's what we forgot. We could have chosen to be a fish."

"Chicken!" said Boots, looking at the chicken nuggets in his paws. "We could have been born a chicken, and ended up in a bun."

"Beef," said Elvis, staring at *his* bit of sandwich. "We could have been born a beef."

The cats tried to think what a beef looked like. Perhaps there were a few more animals in the world that they had forgotten to mention.

"There is a very interesting fact about fish," Marco went on. "Catfish, to be precise. I read it once in the newspaper. Did you know that catfish have whiskers just like we do, and that they can even taste with their tails?"

Now the cats were really staring.

"I never knew that at all!" said Carlotta. "Oh, Marco, you are so smart! So clever! You are the first cat I ever met who could read. Do you think you could teach me?"

"I would be glad to," said Marco. "Maybe sometime we could start with those newspapers in the loft."

Texas Jake drew himself up to his full height there on the wall and hissed. "There's more to life than reading," he said. "There is adventure and courage and strength and cunning. I am ready to announce the Second Great Mystery that Marco and Polo must solve before they can be members of our club."

"I would think they've done quite enough already," said Carlotta hotly.

"Two more," said Texas. "That was the agreement."

"Okay," said Marco, unable to stand the suspense. "Let's hear it."

"The Second Great Mystery," said Texas, "is this: Where does water go when it rains?"

"That's easy," Marco said, feeling relieved. "I've sat at the window and watched many times when it was raining outside. The water slowly sinks into the ground."

Texas shook his head and smiled derisively. "If all the water that ever rained sank into the ground, the earth would squish every time we stepped on it. It would be like walking on a giant sponge. *Some* of the water sinks into the ground, perhaps, but most of it runs along the gutters in the street."

"Well, if you already know, why did you ask?"

"It runs along the gutters in the street and into the hole under the curb at the corner, yes," Texas said. "Now, where does it go after it goes in the *hole? That's* the Second Great Mystery."

Polo had been very glad to hear that the Second Great Mystery had nothing to do with dogs, but now he wasn't so happy. He looked at Marco. Somehow the mysteries that Texas gave them to solve seemed different from the Mystery of Hair, or the Mystery of Rain, or the Mystery of Masters. Mysteries like those could be answered just by lying around thinking about them. Why did the mysteries he and Marco had to solve mean *going* somewhere? *Doing* something?

Nevertheless, Carlotta was watching, and Marco and Polo did not want to be embarrassed in front of her.

"Well," Marco said to his brother, "shall we go, then?" And they set off together toward the street.

10
THE SECOND GREAT MYSTERY

Do you ever get the feeling Texas doesn't like us?" Polo asked when they had gone around to the front of the Big Burger.

"Let's just say that if Bertram had eaten us whole this morning, Texas wouldn't have cried," Marco answered.

"Why doesn't he just tear us to shreds and get it over with?"

"Because fighting upsets Carlotta, and *nobody* wants to upset Carlotta," said Marco.

"So what are we going to do?"

"See where water goes once it's down the hole," Marco told him, and they walked over to the curb. Out in the street, cars were moving slowly through puddles, their windshield wipers going *swick, swack, swick, swack.*

"See there?" said Marco, watching the thin stream of water that was running along in the gutter. A leaf floated by—a stick, a gum wrapper. "The hole is that way."

"How did you figure it out?" asked Polo. "Are holes always north?"

"North has nothing to do with it."

"You always turn to your right to find the hole?"

"Turning right doesn't have anything to do with it either."

"I give up," said Polo.

"Everything was *floating* in that direction, Polo. Water runs downhill."

"It does? Oh, Marco, you're so clever."

As they went along the curb, the sound of water grew louder. At first they heard merely a trickle, but as they came closer to the corner, the trickle became a soft rush, and when they reached the place where the mailbox stood, somewhere, down deep below them, the rush was louder still.

Marco and Polo suddenly grew very quiet. They lowered their bodies close to the ground, tails straight out behind them. Slowly, slowly, Marco crept forward, lifting a front paw and carefully putting it down. Then a hind foot. He thrust his neck far out from his body and wiggled his nose as he sniffed. This was a deep-water smell, a dark smell, an outdoors smell, a *wild* smell.

He crept closer to the edge of the curb where all the water was disappearing and peeped over the side, leaning forward farther and farther, all four legs bunched together on the curb.

"It's the hole," he told Polo, moving backward again.

"What's in it?"

"Darkness."

"What do we do now?"

90

"Go down there and look. Wait until that line of cars passes."

They stood together in the drizzle, their paws wet, fur wet, noses wet, and no matter how Polo tried, he couldn't forget their velveteen basket back home, the plate of canned halibut that Mrs. Neal fed them in the evenings, the bedtime yummies from the little square box, the pats, the coos, the fresh water that Mrs. Neal never forgot to put in their bowl.

"Now!" he heard Marco say. He jumped into the gutter where all the water was going, and—both of them holding onto each other—looked down into the hole.

At first all Polo could see was blackness, but then he could make out a brick ledge off to one side.

Marco saw it too. "Let's jump onto that," he said, pointing. "At least we'll be out of the water, and perhaps we can get a better look at what's down there."

A truck was coming, sending a spray from its wheels, so Marco jumped first, through the opening below the curb and onto the brick ledge; then Polo followed.

The sound of water was very loud here beneath the street and seemed to echo around them. Trapped behind the ledge was a heap of trash—paper cups, pages of newspapers, a shoe, a bottle, a plastic foam cup, some candy wrappers, and an old umbrella. But beyond the ledge was the stream of water that ran down into a tunnel not too far below.

"Well," said Polo. "We know where old umbrellas and shoes and candy wrappers go, but we still don't know what happens to water once it goes in the tunnel."

"Hold my tail while I take a look," said Marco.

91

Polo took hold of Marco's tail, and his brother leaned far, far over the ledge and looked down the tunnel.

It was a long tunnel, with a patch of light coming in farther on. "The water is running in a little stream just in the middle of the tunnel," Marco called back up. "We could walk along the sides where it's dry and go all the way to the end so we can see where the water goes. Then all we have to do is turn around, follow the tunnel back again, jump up to the ledge, and we're home."

Polo saw no reason why it couldn't be done. The jump down off the ledge was not that far, and if they could follow the tunnel without getting their feet wet, why not? At last they would have solved the mystery of where water goes when it rains.

So Marco jumped first, Polo followed, and a moment later, they were making their way down a long, round tunnel, with a thin stream of water running between them. When they reached the patch of light, they discovered it was another opening, just like the one they had jumped into, and water was coming in this one also. Looking far ahead, they could see still another patch of light and were reassured that the street was just above them, that they could jump up on a ledge at any time and leave the tunnel if necessary.

Things sounded very different in the tunnel. When either cat spoke, his voice echoed along the walls. Now and then there were openings from smaller tunnels or pipes that led to who knows where?

"What we've got to do," said Marco, his words bouncing back at him, all hollow-sounding, "is keep going straight ahead, not making any turns, so that when we come back we'll know we're taking the right path."

"But how will we know when to climb back up to the street?" Polo asked. "All the openings and ledges look the same to me."

Marco stopped suddenly. Polo was right. There weren't any street signs down here, any Big Burger restaurant to mark their path. Polo must be smarter than he thought.

"We've got to count," Marco said. "How many openings have we passed so far? Seven?"

"I thought it was five," Polo guessed.

"Well, we'll say six. That's close enough. But from now on we've got to count."

As more water came running through the openings and pipes, the stream in the center of the tunnel seemed to grow a little wider. They had to keep moving up the sides to keep their paws dry.

On and on they went . . . thirteen openings, fourteen openings, fifteen, sixteen. Marco stared anxiously ahead, wondering how much farther they had to go. Polo realized suddenly that they had each climbed halfway up the walls, the water in the center was getting so wide.

There were other noises in the tunnel now that they had not noticed before. Little pit-pats here and pat-pits there, and sometimes Marco thought he heard words, but when he looked over at Polo and said, "What?" Polo said, "I didn't say anything."

Once, when they passed still another tunnel that was emptying even more water into theirs, Polo saw eyes.

"Eyes!" he said to Marco. "Eyes back there in the tunnel. I saw them!"

"What kind of eyes?" asked Marco, hurrying on, for his nose told him that the smells were changing and that they were approaching something new, something different. "Green slanting eyes? Yellow round eyes?"

"Tiny eyes. Beady eyes. Red, I think."

And then there was the unmistakable sound of feet. Dozens of feet, scurrying along, and a low murmur of little squeals, echoing from tunnel to tunnel. "Intruders . . . here in our tunnels . . . cats . . . strays . . ."

Marco and Polo began to run, and the dozens of scurrying feet came faster too, as dozens of little voices chanted:

> Chase them!
> Get them!
> Scratch them!
> Stew them!
> Bite them!
> Claw them!
> Gnaw them!
> Chew them!

It had sounded like only a few running feet at first, then a dozen, then five dozen, then a hundred at least. Something bit Marco on the tail. Something nipped Polo on the hind leg.

"Run!" Marco told his brother. "Faster!"

But the river rats came too:

Stop them!
Whop them!
Knife them!
Wound them!
Cut them!
Chop them!
Fry them!
Spoon them!

There was another sound now that Marco knew was not rats—a faraway, echoing sound of rolling water, rushing water, tumbling water, and, glancing swiftly behind him, over the tails of the rats, he could see a wall of water roaring down the tunnel, sweeping up everything in its path.

Before he could even yell, "Look out!" water filled his mouth, his nose, his eyes. Small bodies smacked against him, as head over paws he tumbled, while water thundered in his ears, on and on, and Marco felt sure he would die.

11
ON THE RIVER

Polo had thought that the gushing, roaring sound he heard behind him in the tunnel was simply more rats—granddaddies, cousins, aunts, and uncles—all coming to help chase him and Marco out of their kingdom under the streets. But before he could turn to make sure, a wall of water, an ocean of water, a *world* of water, kicked him off his feet.

Head over paws, paws over head, tail and whiskers, whiskers and tail—Polo was swept this way and that, rats' bodies, Marco's body, he didn't know which, hitting him in the side as he clawed at nothing in his desperate attempt to stay alive.

And then, just when he felt his lungs would burst, there was daylight and sky as the torrent of water burst from the tunnel, taking Polo with it. He sailed through the air, and with a splutter, a cough, and a gulp, went under again.

Down, down, down. *Thrub, thrub, thrub* went the water in his ears. Then up, up, up, and he found himself on the surface again, Marco some distance away.

Any minute he expected to go under. He knew nothing of water—had only experienced the quick waterfalls that had come strangely upon him when he had tried to go out the Neals' doors, but that was nothing like this. That was over and done with. This was forever.

Still, he discovered that by using his paws he could keep from going under again. But he had little control over where he was going. The current was carrying him swiftly along—him and Marco and branches and leaves and all sorts of things that floated and bobbed. And as if they weren't miserable enough already, Polo realized that the sky had opened up, and it was pouring again.

"Mar-co!" Polo bleated. A slosh of water hit him in the face.

"Po-lo!" came the faint reply.

There were rats in the river too, and they swam much better than either cat, their tails straight out behind them, pointed noses rising up out of the water. But they seemed more interested in staying afloat than in biting the cats. They had, after all, chased them from the tunnel and couldn't have cared what happened to the intruders after that.

"Po-*(blub)*-lo!" came Marco's voice again. "Head for the log."

Polo tried to steer himself in that direction, while Marco moved toward it too. Once there, he almost had his claws in it, but it slipped away. The second time he tried, his claws held.

Dragging his wet body behind him, heavy with water, Polo managed to get up on the log. Marco, on the other side, crawled up too.

But there was no time to rejoice. With Marco clinging desperately to the bark on one end and Polo clinging to the bark at the other, the log rolled and whirled on down the flowing river. As it tipped from side to side in the current, they struggled to stay on, moving forward, then back, meowing loudly, backs arched, the hair rising on their tails.

"Mama!" Polo wailed once in terror, but even he could scarcely hear it. His cry was swallowed up in the noise of the river.

Marco himself had never been so frightened. Things poked up in the water that looked like strange animals. Once a snake swam by, holding its head just above the surface. The log crashed into rocks and spun around, almost knocking him and his brother into the water, then went whirling on downstream at a dizzying pace.

And then, to Marco's surprise, it stopped. The log came to a clump of rocks jutting just above the surface. Bumping against the largest, it could not go around and held fast.

Marco and Polo climbed quickly onto the rock and huddled side by side, weak from fright. Their hind legs ached from dancing this way and that.

For the first time Polo felt really angry. "Now see what you've got us into!" he said. "You and your stories of life on the great outside! Where's this wonderful ranch? Where are the mountains and valleys? All we've got is rain and river."

Marco said nothing.

"What are we supposed to eat out here? Are we going to spend the rest of our lives on this rock?"

For once Marco's voice was timid. "I feel bad enough myself, Polo. Don't make it worse. We'd better not quarrel—all we've got right now is each other."

That was true enough. The rain was still coming down, 'and each cat looked skinny, his fur matted and stringy against his body.

"I think I know what happened," Marco said miserably. "It started to rain again while we were in the tunnel, so that more and more water began to run through the

101

pipes. Finally it all came together into that big wall of water that washed us out."

Angry as Polo was, he still had to admire his brother's intelligence.

"If it hadn't started to rain again," Marco went on, "we could have walked to the end of the tunnel, seen where the water was going, then walked all the way back and climbed up onto the street."

"Wrong!" said Polo. "The rats would have chased us into the river anyway."

That was true.

Marco tried hard to think of something encouraging. "I've read that sometimes rivers run low," he said. "If the water level goes down, there might be other rocks poking up above the surface, and then we could jump from one to another until we reach the bank."

Polo thought that over. "But if water can get lower, it can also get higher, right?"

It was amazing how brilliant Polo was becoming all of a sudden. Marco nodded without speaking. At this very minute the level of water could be rising—*was* rising— and if it rose higher than the rocks, he and Polo would be swept into the water again. If it did not rise but stayed the same, they could be here forever. And if they got back on the log, hoping it would eventually free itself and go on down the river, they could either drift toward the bank where they might get ashore, or they could drown. What to do?

What if the rats saw them stranded out here? What if they crawled up on the rocks and chewed them to pieces, saving their ears as trophies to hang on their walls?

The rain had lightened now, but still the current was fast; the water had a muddy look, as though it had sucked soil from the banks and was churning it up like a milk-shake.

Something moved on the bank. It was a man in hip boots. He walked along with a raincoat over his head, a fishing rod in one hand and a bucket in the other. He glanced out over the river and suddenly stopped and stared.

"Well, I'll be!" Marco heard him say. "Two cats! How in the dickens did they get out there?"

The man watched them for a moment, then put down his fishing rod and bucket and waded out a little way into the river. The water got deeper and deeper around him, and when it almost reached the top of his boots, the man stopped. He leaned forward and stretched out his arms, but was too far away to reach the cats. Finally he turned and sloshed back to shore.

"Meow!" Marco and Polo wailed together. "Don't leave us! Meow! Meow!"

After what seemed forever, the fisherman returned carrying an old board. This time he put down the raincoat before he waded into the water and, reaching out a second time, was just able to rest the end of the board on one of the rocks.

A bridge! A bridge to safety! Two-leggeds were the smartest of all creatures next to cats, Marco thought. He sniffed at the board to be sure it wasn't a flattened dog in disguise. Then, cautiously, he put out one paw to test it, then the other paw, and started across. When he got to the man, the fisherman picked him up and put him on one shoulder. Then he coaxed Polo onto the board. "C'mon, kitty. Water's getting higher. I can't stay out here much longer."

Polo didn't have to be persuaded. He walked the plank, and the man put him on his other shoulder. Then carefully, step by step, he waded back to shore and deposited the cats, one at a time, on the ground.

"If you aren't something!" he said. "Sure would like to know how you came to be out on the river. I'll bet that's some story!"

"You're right," purred Polo, rubbing up against the man's legs, but the fisherman picked up his rod and bucket again and went on down the bank, leaving Marco and Polo to fend for themselves.

It was evening now. If they were back home at the Neals', they would have found a warm place to lie down—next to the heat register, perhaps. They would have licked each other's fur until they were soft and dry. But now all they wanted to do was get away from the river and the rats. They were soaked clear through, and Marco had a tangle of river reeds around his neck. They headed into the woods but were too exhausted to go farther. Marco and Polo collapsed upon the first mossy patch they came to and slept.

When they woke, it was barely light, but in the autumn morning they could see a path in the woods, and, as Marco explained, a path always leads to somewhere. So they set off.

But there were places in the woods where the path divided, one part going one way, the other leading somewhere else. Which to take? At first Marco tried to reason it out, tried to sense direction by sound and smell. But as the day wore on, and he and his brother grew weaker, he could scarcely think at all. When they came to a fork in the path, they simply took the one that seemed easiest, with no other thought than to somehow, sometime, find their way out of the woods.

Once, when they stopped to rest, Marco said, "The problem is, we're hungry."

"I know," Polo panted.

"There's only one thing I can think of to do," Marco told him.

"I know," Polo said again. *Go hunting.*

He didn't know if he was hungry enough yet to kill a mouse—to kill anything at all. But now he had his brother to think about. So while Marco leaned back against a tree, paws over his stomach, Polo set off through the woods, belly low to the ground, nose and tail quivering, and followed a scent.

The scent, it turned out, was a squirrel that led Polo on a merry chase—in and out of bushes, up and down old stumps, over and under a log or two, until at last it scampered high up in the top of a pine tree and left Polo on a branch far below. Polo backed down, so embarrassed he could hardly mew.

But there was no time to be discouraged, because his nose had picked up another smell, a strong, earthy smell. Again his tail went out behind him, again his nose twitched and his belly hugged the ground. Through leaves, through moss, through sticks and weeds, and suddenly he pounced. A small baby mole was trapped in his paws.

Polo stared at the baby mole. Did you put it in a

sandwich? Toast it on a bun? Serve it on the side, with tartar sauce, perhaps?

"Put him *down*, you big bully!" came a voice from the earth, and Polo turned to see a mama mole sticking her head out of a tunnel near a tree. "You ought to be *ashamed* of yourself!" she went on. "Little Oliver was taking his first walk this morning. Hadn't been outside for more than two minutes, and the likes of you comes along to make a meal of him."

The sandwich had a name? Lunch à la Oliver? Polo released the mole at once, but as soon as little Oliver disappeared down the hole with his mama, hunger hit with such force that Polo felt he could eat almost anything at all, even the mama.

When he returned to Marco, he was carrying two brown beetles in his mouth and dropped one at Marco's feet.

"What's *this?*" Marco asked in disgust.

"Breakfast, lunch, and dinner," Polo said. "Eat it."

Marco did. When their meal was over, they started off, and afternoon became evening once again. It was dark among the trees. Tall pines blocked out the sky, which was growing more gray by the minute. There was the smell of moss and fern and dirt and damp. Strange rustlings came from the bushes, strange whisperings from the branches overhead.

What if every kind of animal had its own territory, Marco was thinking, as they bedded down once again. The Royal Order of River Rats; the Rabbit Defense League; the Brotherhood of Squirrels; the Union of Chipmunks; the Amalgamated Moles?

When morning came, Marco knew they had to get out of the woods before night fell. They would not have the strength to go another day without proper food. Once they reached open sky, perhaps they could find their way back to the city. With the reeds still knotted about his neck, Marco dragged his body along the path, Polo behind him, until, at long last, the trees ahead seemed to open up a bit. Then there was a piece of sky, and finally they could tell that the woods was ending. The noises of the forest were replaced by the noise of a highway, and a few minutes later, the cats stepped across a ditch, up a bank, and there they were, near Interstate 270.

Whoosh! A car went by only a few feet from where they were standing.

Whoom! A truck thundered by, and a rush of air knocked Polo off his feet, he was that weak.

"I don't think I can make it, Marco," he said, his mouth dry, eyes half-closed. "Go on without me."

Marco crouched beside him. "You *have* to, Polo. Think of Carlotta."

Polo didn't move.

"Think of the way Texas and the others will laugh if we don't come back."

Polo didn't even stir.

"Think of cheeseburgers with bacon, fried fish sandwiches, and spaghetti with meatballs."

Polo opened one eye, and finally he was on his feet once more and followed Marco down into the tall grass that lined the highway.

Marco stood very still in the grass. He did not smell anything he could name. Did not hear anything unusual.

Did not see any sign that said CITY. But something age-less, passed down from cat to cat, some deep prompting—a gift of his ancestors—told him the way to go.

"To the left!" he said excitedly. "That way!"

Again they started off, as far back from the road as they could. Every so often a truck roared by that was so big, so heavy, so loud, that Polo mewed in fright. They would stop a moment until their shaking subsided, then go on.

Once they came to the body of a black animal with a white stripe that had been run over by a car, and their nostrils twitched with the smell. Another time it was an animal with black fur, like a mask, around his eyes, that had been hit. Marco didn't know what kind of animals they were, but he knew that if he and his brother were not careful, they could be the ones out on the road.

Polo began to sob.

"Be brave, Polo," Marco told him. "Keep your eyes straight ahead, put one paw in front of the other, and we'll get there by and by."

Once again they had to sleep outdoors. They drank a little water from the ditch and made a meal of beetles, but the next evening, long after dark, Marco and Polo finally reached the city. They found the Big Burger res-taurant, found the alley, and, at long last, dragged them-selves to the garage and started up the dusty steps to the loft.

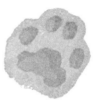

12
IF CATS WERE IN CHARGE

They heard raucous laughter coming from above. Texas Jake was singing a little verse over and over again, and Marco could hear his feet thumping about on the floorboards as he danced:

> They'd be back here if they could.
> Dummy diggle and hi dee dee.
> Those two cats are gone for good.
> Rum pum piddle and a fi fee fee.

"I saw them disappear into that hole myself," said Boots. "Waited a whole hour and never saw another whisker of them." He paused. "I don't know; I sort of liked the stupid one."

Polo felt his tail thicken.

"I sort of liked them both," said Elvis. "We never had a cat in our club before that could read."

"Fair is fair!" said Texas. "They simply weren't equal to the task. Didn't we all have to solve a mystery before we could be admitted to the brotherhood?"

"Carlotta didn't," said Elvis.

"Well, now, Carlotta didn't have to, because Carlotta is . . . um . . . well, Carlotta is *Carlotta*, that's what," said Texas. "Yes, lads, things are going to be back like they used to be, and Carlotta will forget about those two house cats once and for all." And then he sang:

Oh, lickety lie, lickety lole,
Marco and Polo are down in the hole.
Oh, higgledy hay, higgledy hen,
They'll never be near our Carlotta again.

Marco and Polo each put one paw on the top step, and a moment later they stood on the dusty floor of the loft, the tangle of river reeds still wrapped about Marco's neck.

Texas, who was dancing on top of an old trunk, stopped with one paw in the air and slowly, slowly put it down. All the yellow seemed to fade from his face, and he looked as though he were seeing a ghost. Two ghosts.

"They're back!" cried Boots in astonishment.

Marco walked over to Texas Jake and stared him right in the eye: "The river," he said. "The water goes into the hole at the corner, through a long tunnel—miles and miles of tunnel—and into, at last, the river. That is where water goes when it rains."

There was absolute silence as the other cats stared in wonder. Marco and Polo, to be sure, were worth staring at, for the skin on their bodies was visible between the

clumps of wet hair that lay matted against them. They were thinner by far. Their whiskers drooped and their paws were muddy. They smelled of far-off exotic things that Texas, Boots, and Elvis had never known.

Before Texas could open his mouth to speak, there was the sound of pawsteps on the stairs, and then Carlotta hurried into the loft.

"You're back!" she cried joyfully. "Oh, Marco! Oh, Polo! I was so afraid I'd never see you again. But look at you! Where have you been? What happened?"

Then she saw the rat bite on Polo's leg and immediately set to work licking his wound as Marco began his tale of adventure under the streets. Of the dark tunnels, and the perpetual drip-drip of water. Of the red, beady eyes they'd seen in the tunnels, the pitter-patter of feet, the squeals and squalls as the river rats attacked, and finally, the wall of gushing water that washed them—cats and rats alike— into the river.

Carlotta had never seen a river, so Marco had to describe it, with Polo's help. They told how they had almost drowned but had managed to crawl up on a log, which carried them to the rocks, where a two-legged had rescued them. And then—drawn only by a feeling Marco could not explain and the memory of Carlotta's care—they had, at long last, returned with the answer to the Second Great Mystery.

"And you've done it! You've done it!" Carlotta cried, tugging at the reeds around Marco's neck to free him of them, then making his fur all fluffy again. "You've done it magnificently! You've done it splendidly! Oh, Tex, aren't they wonderful?"

If this is heaven, I'm in it, Marco thought.

Texas was up in the top of the coatrack now, draped over one of the spindles, and appeared to be in shock. Elvis and Boots huddled together on the army cot, stunned and silent.

"A banquet!" Carlotta said. "A banquet, everybody! Let's celebrate the safe return of our great explorers. Come on, T. J. Come along, Boots and Elvis."

So down the alley the six cats went to the Big Burger, Texas Jake tagging along in spite of himself. Marco and Polo were served first, of course—all the best delicacies, and when all stomachs were satisfied at last, the cats sat up on the wall.

Polo was watching a man from the restaurant dump another load of leftovers in the garbage, and this reminded him of the fisherman on the bank of the river. "If it hadn't been for the fisherman who rescued us," he mused, "we might not be alive to tell this story."

"Baaaaad fisherman!" Texas Jake muttered, but only Marco heard him.

"Two-leggeds do, from time to time, manage to do something kind," said Carlotta. "Something intelligent, even. It's just that too often they overlook all the nice things *we* do for *them*. Our list of good traits is definitely longer by far than our bad ones. We let them pet us, groom us, comb us, feed us, and what thanks do we get?"

"None," said Boots. "We do not bark and keep the neighbors awake."

"We don't leap up on people when they come in the door," said Elvis.

"We don't act like idiots, running after sticks."

"We don't hang our heads out of automobiles."

"We don't even *like* automobiles."

The list was getting so long it took the cats a full two minutes to sing their own praises.

"But do they ever mention these? No," Texas Jake said, suddenly getting in the spirit of things. "It's what we do wrong that lives after us. They forget that we are cats, and we do what cats generally do. Claws are for scratching, and so we scratch. If *we* were in charge, and *humans* were pets, we'd have a few rules, don't think we wouldn't."

"I wouldn't let them open umbrellas in the house," said Elvis. "Humans will walk in a room on a rainy day, the cat sound asleep on the rug, and all at once they press a button, and *whomp!* Like to scare you out of your skin, that's what."

"I wouldn't let them boil water," Boots whined. "Did you ever notice how a two-legged will put on the teakettle, then make a phone call? The water will boil, the kettle will whistle away, and my ears almost drop off, the pain is so dreadful. But do they ever think about us?"

"Well, *I* wouldn't let them smoke," said Carlotta. "It gets in my fur and I have to wash myself completely to get the odor out. Every time the master reached for a cigarette, I'd say, 'Uh-uh, Peter,' or 'No ciggies,' or 'Have a nice yummy instead.' And if I caught him smoking after I told him not to, I'd lock him in the bathroom. Every time I passed the door, I'd say, 'Baaaad Peter! Bad! Bad! Bad!' "

"If *I* were in charge of humans, I wouldn't let them use the vacuum cleaner," said Texas. "They think it's fun, you know, to sneak up on a sleeping cat. Well, I'd like to sneak up on a sleeping two-legged for once, put the vacuum nozzle against *his* head, and turn the power on. And they wonder why we pee on the rug."

All eyes turned to Marco and Polo. "What rules would you have if *you* were the master?" Carlotta asked.

And both together, Marco and Polo answered: "The car; we wouldn't let them put us in the car."

With that, all six cats began talking at once, and each had his own tale of horror.

"They open the windows so you can hear trucks roaring by on one side, motorcycles on the other," said Carlotta.

"They go off sometimes and leave you there alone, while the car gets warmer and warmer," said Elvis.

"And then, what do you get at the end of the journey?" Boots asked angrily. "A shot in the rump! An ear exam! Why dogs like to ride in cars I've never been able to figure."

"Us either," said Polo. "I think if I had to go in Bertram's yard again, face the rats, and be dumped into a raging river, I'd do all three before I'd ever go inside an automobile."

Nobody saw Texas Jake smile.

The restaurant man was coming out to hose off the trash area again, so the cats scampered back down the alley to the garage and up the steps to the loft.

"Texas," Carlotta said, when the cats were all assembled. "I make a motion that in view of the Two Great Mysteries Marco and Polo have solved, they now be admitted to the club without any further discussion, debate, or ado."

115

"Carlotta," purred Texas, "I am a cat of my word. I said that they have one Great Mystery left to solve, and one Great Mystery it is. When they bring us the answer, they shall be members forever, with all the advantages that membership brings."

"What advantages does it bring?" asked Polo, wondering.

"You get to sleep in the loft, you get Carlotta's company, and you get to eat at the Big Burger without us tearing your ears off," said Texas.

"Oh," said Polo.

Marco was feeling especially strong after the good dinner and all Carlotta's care, so he said, "Just tell us, Tex, and get it over with. What's the Third Great Mystery?"

The other cats turned toward Texas Jake expectantly, and the big yellow cat leaned forward in the rocker.

"The Third Great Mystery," he said, "is this: Where do two-leggeds go when they get in their cars?"

A gasp went around the circle.

"Texas!" cried Carlotta. "No! Don't make them do that!"

"What do you mean, 'Where do they go?' " Marco challenged. "We already know where they go. They go to the vet. You've gone with them. You know."

"But sometimes they get in their cars without us," Tex went on. "Most of the time, in fact. Where do they go then?"

Marco had to admit he had never given it a thought. But then an idea came to him: "To the store," he said. "They go to the store and bring back cat food. You see the sacks yourself!"

Texas Jake smiled just a little. "But sometimes they get in their cars without us and when they come back they do not have any groceries. Where do they go *then?*"

"I don't know," said Marco.

"Well, *that,*" said Texas Jake, "is what you have to find out."

13
THE THIRD GREAT MYSTERY

Marco's first thought was that he would have to say no. His second thought was that even if he said yes, it would be impossible. Cats could jump over a fence into a forbidden yard and they could jump down into a hole, but they could not get themselves into an automobile.

"We *would,*" Marco said, "but how can we get inside a car?"

"Listen to me," said Texas Jake. "Below us, at this very moment, is a car. Every morning Mr. Murphy comes out of the house and gets inside it. Every morning he goes somewhere, and every evening he comes home again. All you have to do is go with him, see where he goes, what he does, and come back and tell us."

Carlotta's tail began to lash back and forth. "That's unfair, Texas! None of the other cats had to do any of these things. If Marco and Polo get in a car, we'll never see them again."

Texas grinned. He couldn't seem to help himself.

"If we *do* go, and we *do* come back, we're members?" asked Marco.

"Absolutely. Like brothers. All for one and one for all," Texas purred.

"How do we get inside the car?"

"Here's how," said Texas. "Murphy's fat, see. He opens the door, slow-ly puts in one foot. He slow-ly slides himself onto the seat and tries to get all of his stomach behind the wheel. Then he slow-ly pulls his other leg in after him and shuts the door. You'll have plenty of time to hop into the backseat while he's getting his legs inside."

"But how will we know they'll really see anything?" Boots protested. "How do we know they won't just hide on the floor until the car comes back again, and make up something?"

"Because," said Texas, "they have to bring back proof that they got out. Then they will have solved the Third Great Mystery—where do two-leggeds go when they don't go to the vet or the grocery store?"

"Done," said Marco. "We'll do it."

Polo began to quake.

"Oh, Marco! Oh, Polo! I'll think of you every minute," Carlotta said, weeping.

It was all for Carlotta, Marco told himself. That's why he and Polo were risking their lives.

There was nothing that could be done until morning when Mr. Murphy got into his car, so the six cats set off once again for the Big Burger. The LOST CATS poster was still up on the telephone pole at the end of the alley, but it was hanging by just one tack now. The rain had smeared the ink so that the letters ran together, and you could hardly tell if the picture was supposed to be two cats or two dogs or what.

Texas jumped up on a trash can behind the restaurant and lifted an empty tuna can in the air. "To the warriors!" he added jovially, and Boots and Elvis joined in: "To our pals."

"I really hate to see you do this," Elvis confided to Polo when they were busily eating. "I must say, I rather like you, though you aren't half as good-looking as I am."

"Somehow we'll make it back," Polo told him, not even believing it himself.

If Texas wasn't so jealous of him because he could read, Marco was thinking, he might even have learned to like the big cat. He noticed that when the usual tribe of kittens came scurrying up to the trash cans, it was Texas Jake that rummaged about for the choice tidbits at the bottoms of the cans and gave them to the kittens. If an elderly cat with arthritis of the hindquarters came by, it was always Texas that leaned down and hoisted him up on the wall. But maybe even big cats, at times, didn't feel quite as big or as wonderful as they looked.

For after-dinner entertainment, Elvis and the cat quartet put on another performance on the wall behind the trash cans. This time, however, the songs were sad—of sailors going off to sea, soldiers going off to war, sons leaving home, and lovers riding off into the sunset.

The Siamese with the blue eyes that sang tenor sniffed just a little when they told him of Marco and Polo's mission, the Persian with the fluffy tail used it to wipe

120

his eyes, and the large Abyssinian with the mournful face had to pause for a moment while he gulped back tears.

Again, a crowd gathered in the parking lot to listen and point to the yowling cats. Some of the people even sat on the hoods of their cars and smiled, and Elvis told the others that he had never sung quite so splendidly, and for such an appreciative audience.

For the final number the cat quartet sang a rousing version of "When Johnny Comes Marching Home Again" as a good-luck song for Marco and Polo:

> Our tab-by cats are off again,
> Hurrah! Hurrah!
> We hope that they behave like men.
> Hurrah! Hurrah!
> Our aunts will cheer, our uncles shout,
> Our kittens they will all turn out,
> And we'll all . . . feel . . . gay . . . when . . .
> Tabbies come march-ing home.

Once more Carlotta broke into tears and rubbed her head against Marco, then Polo. But there was no time for romance or even consolation, because suddenly two men from the restaurant hurried out. One was yelling and waving his arms at the cats; the other carried the hose. A stream of water splashed against the wall and sent the cats scattering in all directions.

"Get out of here, you blasted howlers, and quit raiding our trash cans!" one of the men yelled.

The Siamese, the Persian, and the Abyssinian ran one

way; kittens and strays and old cats ran another. Marco, Polo, Carlotta, Boots, Elvis, and Texas headed for the alley and arrived gasping and panting back in the loft of Murphy's garage.

"See what I mean about people?" said Texas. "You'd think they'd be glad we were giving a free concert for the customers. No appreciation whatsoever."

"Still," said Elvis grandly, admiring himself in an old mirror, "it was the performance of a lifetime. I sang from the soul—from the gut, if you will. My lifelong ambition has finally come true." He turned for his expected kiss from Carlotta, but she was still weeping.

They all fell asleep about midnight. Carlotta insisted on sleeping between Marco and Polo, which ordinarily would have made Polo very happy, but tonight he was just too nervous.

He got up around three, found the string that had been used to tie the newspapers together, and began sucking on one end. Before long, he had swallowed the end, so there was nothing to do but keep eating until the string was gone.

He still felt like sucking, however; he still needed comfort. A fringe on a lampshade was the next to go, and then a ribbon from an old hat.

When the sun came up later and Texas woke everyone with a rousing, "Good morning, lads, and how are we feeling today?" Polo suddenly crouched down in the center of the floor, thrust out his neck, and with a few desperate coughs, threw up the string, the fringe, the ribbon, and the contents of last night's supper.

Carlotta covered her eyes.

"A little sick at the stomach, are we?" gloated Texas Jake.

Polo didn't answer. Just upchucked again.

"A little weak in the knees, perhaps? A little yellow in the whiskers?"

"Polo's fine," Marco answered. "And we're going."

"Good!" said Texas.

While he and Elvis, Boots, and Carlotta peered down from the loft, Marco and Polo hid behind some old tires in one corner of the garage and waited for Mr. Murphy to come out.

"Be brave!" Carlotta meowed when she heard the man coming. "Be quick!"

"Be quiet," said Texas Jake.

Mr. Murphy came in the open end of the garage. He was a big man with an enormous stomach. Just as Texas had told them, Murphy opened the car door and put one leg in. Then slow-ly, he lowered himself down onto the seat, and it was while he was trying to wedge his stomach behind the steering wheel that the cats slipped in through the open door, onto the floor of the backseat, and quietly huddled down in a heap.

Slam. The door closed behind them, and now there was no turning back.

Car keys jingled in the ignition, the motor roared, and a moment later the Chevy with the cats inside backed out of the garage and into the alley.

"Now remember," Marco whispered to Polo, "no matter how terrified we get, how desperately we want to get out, we can't make a sound. Not a mew. Not a peep. If Murphy finds us, he'll open the door and toss

125

us out of the window, and we're road kill. Dead meat. Understand?"

Polo was too terrified to answer. He was always frightened at the vet's office, but even more terrified on his way there and home again. He still remembered the day the Neals brought them home from the Humane Society. As soon as the car had started and the ground beneath them wasn't stable anymore, he and Marco had made such strange whining noises that they looked at each other in surprise. And ever since, when the Neals had taken them to the vet's, noises came from Polo's throat that he didn't even recognize himself.

As the car went faster and the noises on both sides of them grew louder, the cats braced their bodies against each other. Whenever Marco felt a yowl coming on, he pressed one paw against his mouth. Whenever Polo felt a wail about to escape, he grabbed hold of his tail with his teeth.

They closed their eyes as the car swayed back and forth. Up in the front seat, Mr. Murphy began to sing:

Oh, bury me not on the lone prairie,
These words came low and mournfully
From the pallid lips of a youth who lay
On his dying bed at the close of day.

Marco listened. He wasn't sure, but it sounded a bit like a cowboy song, and cowboys, he knew, lived on ranches.

Oh, bury me not on the lone prairie
Where the wild coyotes will howl o'er me,

126

Where the rattlers hiss, and the crow flies free,
Oh, bury me not on the lone prairie.

It *was* a cowboy song! Now Marco was sure of it. Maybe Murphy was a cowboy! *Maybe,* in fact, he was driving west to a ranch. Maybe *that's* where the two-leggeds went when they weren't going to the vet or the grocery store. If so, maybe this whole horrible ride would not be in vain.

Whoom! A diesel truck roared by. What Marco was afraid of was that he would be sick in the car. He felt his stomach rumble. He had never told Polo, but what he missed even more than his velveteen basket was his litter box, and clean litter that was changed every day. He knew he had the whole wide world now to do his business in, but there were bugs and worms in the dirt, and he always got his paws muddy. Still, better dirt than the backseat of the Chevy where, if he did his business now, Murphy would surely notice.

"Oh, bury me not—" and his voice failed there;
But we took no heed of his dying prayer;
In a narrow grave just six by three,
We buried him there on the lone prairie.

Mr. Murphy's singing was almost as bad as his driving. His voice went up and down, and the car went weaving along. Finally—after what seemed days, weeks, years in the car—the automobile began to slow down, then to bump along over rough ground, and finally came to a stop. The door opened and even before Mr. Murphy put one leg out, the cats tumbled from the car and darted beneath it.

And then, peeping out from between Murphy's feet, Marco could scarcely believe what lay before him.

14
A Fight to the Finish

It was the strangest landscape they had ever seen. No trees, no houses, no grass. Just acres and acres of reddish brown dirt. There were huge mounds of it here and there, and tire tracks that descended into the deep spaces in between.

Polo stared. "A ranch?" he asked in astonishment.

"It must be!" said Marco. "Yes, I'm sure of it! Polo, we made it! We did it!"

At last something was going right. After all of this—the Grand Escape, the water hose, Bertram the Bad, the rats, the river—they had found what they were looking for. A place to spend their lives.

"If only Carlotta were here," Marco said. "Those are the hills." He pointed to the mounds of dirt. "And those are the valleys." He pointed to the spaces in between.

From their hiding place under the Chevy, they saw

Mr. Murphy go up to a group of men. They were all wearing yellow hats on their heads.

"See? See?" Marco said excitedly. "All cowboys wear hats. I read that somewhere."

"Where's the horse?"

"I don't know. It'll show up pretty soon, I imagine," Marco answered.

The men stood about talking for a few minutes. Then some put on work gloves. Some picked up shovels. Some went one way and some went another, but Mr. Murphy went straight ahead to a large orange creature that had been keeping very still in the background. It had a very long neck and it sat with its paws tucked under.

Marco and Polo stared. Mr. Murphy climbed on top of it, sat down, and suddenly the creature roared. It gave a gigantic *vroom* sound, then slowly turned its head, its neck swiveling about, its jaws wide open, and gulped up a big mouthful of dirt.

"The . . . the *horse!*" Marco said. "Now we know! A horse is a huge orange creature with a long neck, a gigantic head, and a large mouth with teeth, and it eats dirt."

"So what do *we* eat?" Polo wondered aloud. "Where do we sleep? What do we *do* on a ranch?"

"All I know is that ranches are wonderful because cowboys sing about them all the time," Marco explained.

"Murphy was singing about dying and getting buried," Polo reminded him.

"Well, maybe things are better beyond the bend," Marco said. "Let's get away from the horse and look around."

Stepping behind a mound of dirt, they followed the tire tracks down to another huge space below, but it all looked the same. No trees, no houses, no grass—just mountains and mountains of dirt.

Marco looked up at the clouds. "Well, anyway," he said, "it's the land of the Big Sky."

"We can't eat sky. We can't eat dirt," Polo told him.

It *was* disappointing, Marco had to admit. In truth, he had never seen a mountain or valley in his life. But he had certainly expected more than this.

So finally he and Polo did what they always did when they were bored or hungry or disappointed: They went to sleep. They found a giant hill to hide behind, and then, warmed by the sun, fell into a deep, deep slumber.

Polo dreamed that the horse had seen them. He dreamed that not only had it seen them, but it was coming to gobble them up. Louder and louder, closer and closer, and just as he was telling himself to wake up, he felt the earth give way beneath him, and realized it was a dream no longer, that he and Marco were high in the air, carried in the jaws of the giant horse.

"M-m-marco!" Polo meowed, closing his eyes.

"P-p-polo!" Marco said, peering over the side.

"Good-bye," said Polo. "I forgive you for talking me into running away and ruining my life."

"Good-bye," said Marco. "If by any chance you survive me, give my tail to Carlotta, to remember me by."

The next they knew, the giant horse had spit them out on top of a mountain of dirt. They went rolling, tumbling, somersaulting down the heap, their mouths, ears, noses, and eyes filled with reddish brown soil.

When they came to rest at last some distance away, Polo
tested every part of his body before he opened his eyes. His
back legs worked. His front legs worked. His paws. His tail.
His tongue. Slowly he raised his head and looked for Marco.
His brother was crawling toward him. He looked like a cat

made of clay. If Polo hadn't been so miserable himself, he would have laughed. But there was dirt and dust everywhere. No water to wash in. No water to drink.

Dirty, disgusted, and desperately thirsty, the cats found their way back to the Chevy, hid in the shade beneath, and, for the rest of the day, watched Mr. Murphy ride the giant animal that ate dirt and spat it out; ate and spat it out. Marco didn't think he had ever seen a more useless creature in his life, and now he knew that it was all lies about ranches. Cowboys went there and died, that's what.

When Mr. Murphy got back into the car again, the cats were back inside too, quick as a wink. They did not mew as they went home. They did not cry or even whisper, did not whimper or whine. And finally, when the Chevy rolled into the garage, Marco and Polo, tired and filthy, jumped out when Mr. Murphy opened the door. As soon as the large man had gone inside his house, they drank some rainwater that had collected inside an empty hubcap, then started upstairs.

The other cats were waiting. Peering over the edge of the loft, their eyes grew huge when they saw the tabbies return. Texas Jake could say nothing, nothing at all.

"Marco! Polo!" Carlotta cried, rushing to meet them. "Oh, you've come! You've come! And look what they brought back with them, Texas. Dirt!"

While Marco and Polo told their tale of the ranch and their narrow escape from the jaws of the giant horse, Carlotta immediately set to work cleaning their ears. Texas and the others listened in awe. Marco and Polo: the cats that could not die. If they said they had been to a ranch, then it must be so. If they said they had faced certain death in the mouth of a giant horse, then that also was gospel truth. They had come back with the answer to the Third Great Mystery: When two-leggeds were not heading to the vet or the grocery store, they went to a ranch to be cowboys.

Suddenly Marco sat up and sniffed. Then Polo. Carlotta stopped licking. Something odd was in the air. Something scary. The other cats smelled it too. Polo felt his tail thicken. Marco felt the hair on his back stand straight up.

And then they heard it—the noise, the growl, the yelp, the bray that could mean only one thing: Bertram the Bad was on the loose.

There was the rapid thud of paws in the alley, the clink of a chain being dragged. Someone was yelling, and there was the sound of running feet. But Bertram the Bad was unstoppable. He had picked up the cats' scent in the Murphys' garage, and was already on his way up the stairs.

The six cats scattered, their hair standing on end. A moment later the huge mastiff lunged into the loft.

"Climb up! Get away!" Texas yelled to the others. Carlotta leaped to the coatrack, Boots to a window ledge, Elvis to a card table, Polo to a lamp, and Marco to a bookcase. Texas alone stayed in the middle of the floor to fight off Bertram.

There was a hiss, a yelp, a cry, as a blur of rolling fur moved across the floor. From his place on the bookcase high above, Marco tried to determine what was what as the monstrous ball of paws and hair came rolling back the other way.

The air was filled with snarls, grunts, growls, hisses, yelps, cries, and barks. For a moment the big mastiff stopped, his snout bleeding, and Texas tried to leap on his back. But Bertram was too fast for him and soon had him by the neck, shaking him back and forth like a rag mop. Carlotta shrieked.

And then Marco's eye fell on Bertram's old sock, and he leaped down onto the cot, picked up the sock in his mouth, and, giving it a swat with one paw, sent it flying by the mastiff's nose and on down the steps to the garage below. Bertram went after it, just as his master entered the garage and grabbed him by the collar.

It had happened so fast and was over so quickly that the cats were still in shock. The loft was in shambles, fur everywhere. Slowly Marco looked around to see if everyone was all right.

Carlotta was high on a shelf, trembling. Boots was still on the window ledge, shivering. Polo was dry mouthed and shaking on the army cot, but Elvis crouched over Texas Jake, who lay on his side in the middle of the floor.

Marco saw the big yellow cat whisper something to Elvis, his sides heaving as he labored to breathe. Then the big cat lay still.

The other cats sank down on their haunches, tails still bushy with fright, fur in disarray, eyes huge, mouths half-open, breathing shakily. And then Carlotta began to weep. Boots and Elvis too wiped their eyes.

"I can't believe it," Carlotta sobbed. "Not Texas!"

"If . . . if only he had jumped up here with us," said Boots.

"One minute more and Bertram's master would have

taken him home," Elvis gulped, and the weeping went on. Boots had to excuse himself to go outside. Elvis turned his back to the others and stared out a window. Nobody mentioned how Marco had gotten rid of the dog by throwing Bertram's sock down the stairs, because this was a time for thinking of Texas.

At last Boots came up to the loft again, and all the cats formed a circle around their fallen leader.

"He . . . he was a good ole cat," said Elvis, bowing his head.

"If you walked up to T. J. and asked him to lick behind your ears, he'd stop whatever he was doing and lick until you didn't itch anymore," added Elvis. "He was just that kind of cat."

Marco and Polo listened as the stories went on: how Texas Jake fought off a raccoon twice his size. How he once rescued a kitten that had fallen into a bucket of water. There were stories of how he had jumped on a stray dog's back and ridden him out of the alley, and about the night he chased a weasel. But Bertram the Bad had been too much, even for T. J.

"He tried to protect us," Carlotta cried. "T-t-texas had his faults, but he defended us with his life."

"What were his last words, Elvis?" Marco asked softly.

"He asked me to look after his wife and kittens," Elvis replied.

Carlotta stopped crying. "He had a *wife* and *kittens?*"

"Somewhere," said Elvis.

The cats continued to sit around their hero.

"He should be buried with a little something from all of us," Carlotta said. "Just to show our love and appreciation. When I go home, I'm going to get my ribboned collar and bring it back."

"I put aside a bit of bird the day before yesterday," Boots told them. "I could get that, perhaps."

"My owner has a picture of me sitting on the grand piano. I'll bring that tomorrow to be buried along with him," said Elvis.

When the cats turned to Marco and Polo, Marco simply walked across the loft, picked up the river reeds that had been tangled about his neck, and he and Polo laid them gently, like a wreath, by the big cat's nose.

And then, one of the yellow cat's eyes opened. Marco and Polo stared.

"I've got nine lives, lads, and this was only one of them," Texas Jake said.

"He's alive!" cried Carlotta. "Oh, T. J., is it really true?"

"W-w-we thought you were dead! We were *sure* you were dead!" said Elvis.

"Well, half-dead anyway," said Texas. "I was stunned there for a while." He winced as he tried to sit up. "This will mean a trip to the vet for sure and a couple weeks of rest at home. But I'll be back in this clubhouse, don't you worry."

And so, dragging his injured body, Texas Jake moved slowly down the stairs—cats ahead of him, behind him, and on either side to make sure he got home okay. When he had been delivered safely to a white house across the alley, Carlotta said that the rest of them should go to the Big Burger to regain their strength after all they had been through. The five cats set off.

There was no more cat poster on the telephone pole. The wind had blown it down and away, but the air was filled with the aroma of frying fish. Marco, who had developed a taste for tartar sauce, was wondering whether he should have an appetizer of sirloin first, or perhaps a bit of cheese and bacon, when he saw the Siamese, the Persian, and the Abyssinian walking toward them.

"Bad news," all the cats said at once.

"What's yours?" asked the Siamese.

"Texas Jake was hurt in a fight with Bertram the Bad," said Elvis. "He is on his way to the vet."

The Siamese, the Persian, and the Abyssinian shook their heads sadly.

"What's yours?" asked Carlotta.

"Come and we'll show you," said the Siamese. And they all entered the parking lot of the Big Burger.

The building was still there, topped by its red-and-yellow sign. But back by the wall where the trash cans had stood, there was a big blue Dumpster, with a hinged door, tightly closed. And on the side of the Dumpster, someone had written a message with chalk.

"What does it say?" the other cats asked, turning to Marco.

And Marco read it aloud: "There is no such thing as a free lunch."

15
HOME?

It suddenly seemed as though all the cats had a most pressing reason to go home.

Elvis said that mice had been making a nest on his master's back porch, so he, of course, was needed.

Boots said he had an old aunt living two doors down, and it was time he paid her a visit.

The Siamese, the Persian, and the Abyssinian had housekeeping chores to attend to, and finally it was just Marco, Polo, and Carlotta left in the parking lot behind the Big Burger.

"I suppose," said Carlotta, "that I ought to be going too."

Polo looked very sad. "I'd always hoped," he said, "that I would discover that *you*, Carlotta, were my mother."

"I beg your *pardon?*" the she-cat said icily, but when she saw that Polo's heart was breaking, added more kindly, "I'm too young to be your mother, Polo, but you can *think* of me as your mother forever and ever, if you like." She licked his nose. "Remember to wash behind your ears," she told him.

Marco discovered that he had tears in his own eyes. "I feel I've failed you, Carlotta," he said. "You told us once that you would accept a mouse as a token of our gratitude, and we never brought you so much as a whisker. Now I can't even offer you a tidbit from the Big Burger."

"Never mind," Carlotta told him. "There are other trash cans, you know."

"But will we see you again?" asked Marco.

"I'm sure of it. When the moon is full, come looking for Elvis, Boots, and me. And when Texas is well again, the club will go on. It must. Perhaps then you can teach me to read." She kissed them both. "Good-bye," she said. "May you always be quick and brave and wonderful." And then she was gone.

Marco and Polo looked at each other.

"I'm so dirty you could grow flowers in my fur," said Marco.

"I'm so hungry I could eat my own foot," said Polo.

"Let's go home," Marco said at last.

Home.

It was, Polo decided, the most beautiful word in the English language. It was a word that meant love. A word that meant food. A word that meant bed and sunlight coming through the window and someone to brush your fur and change your litter and, yes, even to take you to the vet when you were sick.

They hurried to the far end of the alley in the direction

of the Neals' house. Marco had lost track of time. He did not know what day or week or month it was, but from the look of the sky, it appeared to be early evening. Mrs. Neal would be thinking about dinner soon. She would get a pan to boil the potatoes in and another to cook the meat. She would set the table while the cats watched from the rug in the next room, and at some point, she would turn to them and say, "Well, fellas, how about supper?"

Then they would hear the wonderful music of the can opener, and they would rub against her legs, pledging love and devotion always, and finally she would spoon the food into their porcelain dishes, and Marco and Polo would eat.

The two cats entered the back gate of the Neals' yard. They saw the light in the window and began to smile. They scurried quickly up the walk and Marco began to purr.

Even out on the back porch they could smell a pot roast. Dinner was already on! They could hear the clink of knives and forks as Mr. and Mrs. Neal ate.

"Meow!" cried Polo.

"Meow! Meow!" cried Marco.

The clinking stopped.

"Do you hear cats?" came Mrs. Neal's voice.

"It sounds like it's coming from outside," said Mr. Neal.

"It is! It's us! Your own true-blue kitty cats!" wailed Polo piteously.

A chair scraped against the floor, and there were footsteps as the Neals came to the door.

Marco stood up on his hind legs, he was so eager to get inside.

"Why, it's . . . it's Marco and Polo!" cried Mr. and Mrs. Neal together.

"Yes, yes, it's us! It's us returning home!" Marco purred.

"Let us in! Let us in!" mewed Polo.

"Where on earth have they been?" said Mr. Neal. "Has someone been feeding them, do you imagine?"

"How did they get so filthy?" Mrs. Neal exclaimed.

"Meow!" both cats wailed indignantly. "We're hungry! Let us in! Feed us! Love us!"

The door swung open, and Marco and Polo rushed in. Their purrs sounded like water bubbling in a teakettle as the Neals stooped down to pet them.

"Poor bedraggled things!" said Mrs. Neal.

"Hungry and tired, I'll bet," said her husband.

The cats rubbed up against the Neals' legs. They made a tour of the kitchen to see if any small piece of roast beef had accidentally fallen on the floor. They trailed into the next room to sniff the place out.

There was the velveteen basket, as usual, and there, inside, were two brown-and-white kittens. The kittens sleepily raised their heads as Marco and Polo stared in astonishment.

"Marco and Polo," said Mr. Neal, "this is Jumper and Spinner. Kittens, these are our two explorers, Marco and Polo, returning home."

"Hissss!" went Marco, arching his back.

"Hissss!" went Polo, flattening his ears.

"Mew!" said the two small kittens, turning up their

noses. Then they put their heads on their paws again and settled back down in the basket.

"Now I want all of you to get along together," Mrs. Neal said. "No fighting, no biting, no scratching, no chasing, no taking each other's food."

How *could* they? Marco wondered, still in shock. This is *our* basket, *our* dishes, *our* food!

Leave home for one minute and they find someone else, thought Polo.

But Mrs. Neal had gone back to the kitchen to open

some cat food, and finally two aluminum pie plates were placed on the floor. It was an indignity to eat off pie plates, but for now Marco and Polo were too hungry to care and hurriedly gulped down their supper.

Mr. Neal leaned back in his chair and looked the two cats over. "I suppose Marco and Polo are indoor-outdoor cats now," he said. "They'll never be content again just staying inside."

"They probably want to go back out this very minute," said Mrs. Neal.

"Not right now, we don't," purred Polo, washing his paws.

Marco strolled into the living room. He put one paw in the velveteen basket where the kittens were sleeping.

"Marco!" came Mr. Neal's stern voice behind him.

Marco took his paw out of the basket and looked at Mr. Neal, then at Polo. "We've got trouble," he said, and crouched down in the corner.

Mrs. Neal took cornstarch and brushed it through their fur, until at last Marco and Polo looked like the two sleek cats they had always been. But after the Neals went upstairs for the night, the kittens got up.

"My toy!" Jumper hissed when Polo approached the catnip mouse.

"My water!" Spinner growled when Marco went for a drink from the porcelain bowl.

"*Our* basket!" the kittens mewed together when Marco and Polo tried to lie down.

At last, however, Jumper tired of the catnip and tossed it to Marco. "You can play with it now," he said.

"Oh, no, thank you," said Marco. "We have been so many places and seen so many things that, well, to tell the truth, a toy mouse just isn't the same."

Spinner stopped chasing his tail. "The same as what?"

"The same as real mice scuttling down an alley, of butterflies flitting over your head. Of bees buzzing and birds singing and all the wonderful smells and sounds of the great outdoors."

"We've seen that," Jumper said. "We've seen all that from the window."

"Ah, but it's not the same as being out there yourself. You ought to try it sometime."

"We can't."

"Why not?" asked Marco.

"Because we're indoor cats."

"So were we, once."

"But every time we try to go out, a huge waterfall comes from the sky," Spinner told them.

"Then you must try the side door," Marco said, and explained about Mr. Neal taking things in and out of the basement.

The kittens stared.

"It's true. You can be out in a flash," said Polo, and he told them about their Grand Escape—hiding under the bush, running behind the shed. Marco told them about the mouse Polo had caught in the alley, and every time the two cats stopped for breath, the kittens cried, "Tell more! Tell more!"

"My throat's so dry I can barely talk," said Polo.

"Drink some water!" Spinner said. "Please help yourself from our bowl."

Marco and Polo drank from the porcelain bowl. Then they told about the Club of Mysteries, the cat quartet, and how they had feasted at the Big Burger on delicacies that far surpassed anything the Neals might give them.

"I'm just too tired to talk anymore," Marco said at last. "We need to sleep before we can go on with the story."

"You can have our bed!" the kittens said. "Please sleep so you can tell us the rest."

So Marco and Polo climbed in the velveteen basket. They slowly turned around and around, pawing gently with their feet. They licked each other's heads and finally settled down in their favorite positions.

"Tomorrow," Marco purred to the kittens, "we shall tell you about Bertram the Bad. And the day after that about tunnels under the streets. The day after that it will be a tale of rats and rivers, and after that of mountains and valleys and a beautiful cat named Carlotta."

"Sleep well," the kittens said.

"We shall," the tabbies told them.

And when the Neals got up the next morning, Marco and Polo were sound asleep in the velveteen basket, while the kittens, crouched by the picture window, were plotting the Grand Escape.